THE DRIVER OF SERPENTS

THE DRIVER OF SERPENTS

THE BLESSED & POSSESSED
BOOK ONE

JAY REQUARD

For my Family

PART I

THE SAINT

1

SESSION ONE

Since you're listening, I'll start at the beginning.

In the beginning, when God created the heavens and the earth—

Kidding. Let me start again: this began in New York.

I took a hit off the joint before the busboy opened the back door, the blueberry smoke filling my lungs. I blew it out like a dragon.

Or at least I thought I looked like a dragon. For all I knew, the bloody fool gaped with a curiosity born less from how much smoke I exhaled than the sight of a skinny Irish priest sparking a joint in the middle of a Chinatown alley.

I was still in my blacks I had worn during my final visit to Vatican City—where I had quit less than twenty-four hours before—and I had left my unbuttoned white clerical collar sticking out of my black shirt's proper one.

Fuck, I didn't care. Ex-priest.

My name's Patrick. Saint Patrick of Ireland in case there was confusion later on.

Yes, that one—the Driver of Serpents, Delver of Purgatory, and your favorite disappointment's best reason to get plastered every March.

3

And that night I was about to exorcise a demon in the freezer of an old, dirty Chinese restaurant.

The joint still glowed as I rested it in the gutter for later, my head lightened to the point where I no longer cared about the hangover I had carried all the way from JFK. Sticky from years of grease, sweat, and steam that had browned and bubbled pieces of the paint, the dingy gray door opened with a pop. The smell of boiled cabbage, soggy pepper, and God knows what else struck me as I entered an industrial kitchen, the stainless appliances stained beyond repair. Grimy woks burned over blue gas flames, unmanned by the two cooks crowding one of the kitchen's corners. They puffed on bent, shriveled cigarettes they shared from the same pack of Camels.

The door to the walk-in freezer lay shut, crates of unwashed radishes stacked before it.

I thumbed at the hunk of steel. "There, lads?"

One of the cooks nodded, liver-spotted hand shaking while he drew another lungful of cancer.

The busboy unstacked the crates before the freezer door while I removed my tools from the black peacoat I had worn over my holy monkey suit. Same shit every time—the Good Book, my crucifix, my rosary, and what remained of my vestment, a long scarf of green cloth embroidered in gold knotwork formed to match the silver cross attached to the rosary. Real Irish folk hate it when it's called a "Celtic Cross," as if the bloody sheep-fuckers in Scotland didn't have Druids and shit too, or bless their hearts, problems with those damned limey fucks like everyone else does.

Let me tell you about ancient Ireland and its neighbors: there were Druids everywhere. Tree-hugging, human-sacrificing, wild-ass magic druids.

Then they became Catholics.

That's when the real troubles started.

I let the thought go when I threw on my vestment, kissing the ends before crossing myself. "Any of you got a bottle of water I can use?"

One of the cooks, the younger of the pair, puttered to the front of the restaurant and returned with a bottle of Deer Park, its paper label half-torn from rough handling.

Condensation on the plastic wet my hand, a sensation I do not like when stoned to the gills. "Ah, fuck," I muttered, blessing the water quickly before nodding to the busboy. "Crack her."

The busboy hesitated, checking with the older cook. The man nodded, his fu manchu wet at the ends.

The freezer opened. A putrid smell wafted out, dried by the frost. I walked in, not hesitating for a second—demons are all show-and-tell, very little substance. I could get into the fact that not a single one of these dark bastards would ever actually dig their claws into anybody without God's express permission, but that's a book within itself. Multiple books.

He sat in a folding chair, the kind one saw at wrestling shows, dead center in the small ten by fifteen-foot rectangle. Wrinkled chickens hung from hooks beside slathered beef ribs and trays piled with frozen dumplings, fresh from the packaging discarded in the room's corners. Barefoot, he leaned like a drunkard, the front of his wife-beater stained in blood and grease. The demon had bitten open his bottom lip.

"You speak English?" I asked as the door closed behind us. The lock clacked shut on the outside.

The fluorescent lights revealed enough when he looked up at me. His eyes were blacked out.

My rosary wrapped around my left hand; I twirled the black wooden crucifix in the fingers of my right. I placed it on his knee. "Our Father, who art in heaven..."

"He's not."

"Oh ho! Speaking on the first go!" I stepped back and smiled. Those black eyes stared ahead at the corner of the freezer. "Come on, now. Don't get nervous on account of little ol' me."

The demon said nothing.

I touched his shoulder with the cross. "Hear in the name of God, tormentor, for the one that made this vessel and its waters has come. In the name of Michael of the Archangels, Protector of Heaven, Earth, and the Towers, I beseech thee to speak your name and depart back to Perdition."

The possessed cook's face twitched. He coughed.

Demons lie. That's the first rule, but the tricks were always the same. Keep quiet until the deed is done for whatever the Devil had sent them for. Yet none ever counted on a demon's pride. It must have been a hard fall from Heaven to stay that angry about it.

"Out, vile thing, for the light of the Lord has come with the voice of Mary in our ears." I kept the cross on his shoulder. "Come, fallen child—lose yourself of this flesh, and travel back to your burning place until the slag is gone. Until the day you are judged, leave and begone forever."

The demon raised his head and looked right at me. "We met in Italy, you know."

I belted him across the face, the beads of my rosary biting into my knuckles.

Knocked to the floor, the demon kicked away, a blackened hand out to stop me. "Please, Saint Patrick, please!"

"Is that fucking you, Beherit?" I almost dropped my Bible. "I told you to stop fucking around with souls back in Rome."

He cocked a black eye at me, a small smile on his bloody lips. "You still came."

I unscrewed the cap to my holy water and blessed that son of a bitch right then and there.

No steam, no boiled flesh, but I got what I wanted. The little cook's body writhed and bucked, arms and legs bent at odd angles while the demon convulsed.

Beherit shrieked like dying children.

I squatted at his trembling feet, letting my green and silver rosary dangle from my hand. "Let's cut the shit, boyo." I got his attention, our eyes locked again. "You remember what you said the last time I forced you out of someone?"

"The New Word is still without a body," the demon mumbled, fighting the words. "And the Word resides in her."

"No, no, no—you said come to New York and I would save more

souls. You horned fucks don't talk about saving souls, but I came to New York. Your turn. What's next?"

Beherit scooted to the freezer's wall and leaned against it face-first it like an Egyptian praying on the day the frogs fell. Heaving to steady his racked, wet body, he twisted at the waist to face me, crunching the cook's spine.

"Cut that out," I said.

"I'm getting to it." Vertebrae popped when he aligned his torso to his lower half and rested against the scummed iron. "Do you have a cigarette?"

I rose to my feet. "I don't do tobacco."

"Well, fuck." Beherit searched the red floor in vain. "Care to share the rest of that weed in your boot?"

The cover of my Bible ripped open, my fingers digging through until I found the right passage. "You ever hear the one about Christ in the wilderness?"

"Peace, potato-eater." The demon held his hand up. The veins beneath the cook's skin had darkened, the possession asserted fully over the host's soul. Who knew how long Beherit had kept his claws in this one? I fought him well over a bloody year back in Rome before he started spouting his "New Word" nonsense from a little girl's mouth. Until it stopped sounding like nonsense.

He might have had this poor sod for years.

"Talk, demon." I sipped from my bottle of holy water, easing the parch in my throat. "Be quick."

"'She is here," he said. "She's here in New York."

"Who?"

"And the Word resides in *her*," he quoted again.

We stared at each other for a long time, neither saying anything.

The cross in my left hand, Bible in my right, the answer to my dilemma came swift. "Beherit, I beseech you..."

"Just ask me to leave."

The request startled me. Demons fought, screamed, shouted, but they never gave up until someone broke them like God had. "Why?"

"Why what?" he asked. "Just send me home."

"In the name of Christ and his angels, go back to Perdition, Beherit, and wait for the day of judgment."

The darkness in the cook's eyes subsided, and for a moment, the man tilted his face skyward, as if beyond the moldy green ceiling there lay the sun shining bright upon him for the first time. She was there, I knew, as she always was: Our Mother saving the lambs as her son, the shepherd, had saved us from our sins.

The cook spoke in his language, which I think was Mandarin. I don't know what he said, but I picked out the name "Mary" well enough. I blessed him, provided him the Body and Blood, and had the entire staff recite the Lord's Prayer and way too many Hail Marys to make sure before I got the fuck out of there.

The city glittered, well past midnight, but bustling in the streets outside the alleys. Like Rome, this city never slept, and, like Rome, what went on was no more and no less holy. People marched to work, dumb and blind to the great war within and around them.

I found the leftover of my joint on the curb, and with enough scratch to create a decent little ember. The blueberry hit smooth as I removed my vestment and repacked my gear in my coat.

My phone buzzed.

The Chair had called fifteen times in the last hour.

Letting the grass take away the exhaustion in my neck, back, and hands, I let the city's light bathe me in neon and fluorescents, one lost saint in the places between.

And the Word resides with her.

Whatever the fuck that meant.

2

UBER

The Uber pulled up to the curb not too far of a walk from Chinatown.

"Hi, Patrick, I'm Tina," said the driver, a pretty Latina from some place down below the equator. She spoke perfect English, the telltale sign of a city-native who knew how to switch tongues when needed.

"Hi, Tina, I'm Patrick," I said as I opened the rear passenger side door of her gunmetal Corolla. The inside smelled nice and new, a peculiar detail out of place, along with the attractive driver dressed to the nines in a black pencil-skirt dress and cream blouse well before dawn. This set me off for some reason.

"Late night for a drive, Patrick," she said as I buckled up. "New to New York or just out and about tonight?"

"Oh, I've been here a time or two," I said, forcing pleasantness. The refractory period after an exorcism always left me drained, and the weed didn't help as much as it numbed. "Just out on business."

"Pardon me for asking, but I noticed your accent. Are you here from Ireland?"

"Rome, actually." It was then I noticed how deeply to the side I had slouched against her back window, lost in the folds of my coat. I smoothed out the front of my jeans before straightening up in the seat. "I came in from Rome this evening."

"Oh, really? JFK or La Guardia?"

"Not JFK."

She giggled at the lie, flashing her gaze at me in the rearview for a moment before returning her attention to the road. "So what do you do, Patrick?"

I rubbed my tired, sinful eyes. "I'm an exorcist."

The car quieted, the thrum of the tires on the pavement a lonesome song between us. I used this often as a way to get left the fuck alone. The less who knew me, the better off they ended up, dying in their beds next to their loved ones, going on to the grace of Heaven or whatever they made for themselves afterward. Nine out of ten usually shut their traps until they dropped me off.

The rest often ended up in body bags.

"Are you a priest?" Tina asked. "I noticed the collar."

Damn it, Tina.

"Not anymore."

"Not anymore?" she asked, a smile in her voice.

"Yeah, not anymore," I replied, chuckling on instinct. Pretty girls often made me do stupid shit.

She glanced at her phone mounted on the dash, the GPS letting us know we still had twenty minutes to go before Brooklyn. "And you exorcise demons?"

"Every faith performs exorcisms. I've done a spirit here and there, a monster here and there when called."

"But you exorcise demons," she repeated, a statement this time.

"Yeah, lass. Demons." I patted the front of my coat, feeling the outline of my weed still in the breast pocket. Relieved I had not left it in the bathroom at Kennedy, I eased into a more comfortable position on the bench.

"So, do you believe in angels and demons?" she asked.

"Can't have one without the other."

"But you think they're real."

No, I was just bullshitting! Got me, girl. "Aye, lass."

"Oh, aye, lass," she repeated under her breath in the best brogue she mustered. Her smile broadened. "Are you serious?"

I said nothing, letting the miles eat up the time between us. Civilians didn't like the truth. Less said, the better.

"Do they have horns?"

"Not on this plane," I said, sighing at the futility of it. I hit her full force. "Demons reside in Perdition with Lucifer and Satan, working their way into our souls through the vices of sin and seduction. They may possess us, mind and body, and work at corruption in their drive to further themselves, and therefore all things, from God's grace—but they are never flesh. At least not from what I've seen."

"Oh." Tina hummed. "And you remove them from people's souls?"

"I help the possessed do it for themselves. No one is freed but by their own will."

"Is that from the Bible?"

I fought the urge to reach into my coat and pull out my phone, anything to end the conversation. Yet there was something there, in that moment, between me and some random goddess in New York struggling to make a few extra ducats on the side of whatever she would do when morning arrived. She could have been on the Street, or a stripper on the street. One never knew in this city.

But the urge did not bite at me bad—pretty girls and stupidity, after all. "Some. There's no difference between angels and demons. The latter came when they fell from the former."

"Why did they fall?"

"Why does anyone fall?" Blocks passed by outside my window. Centuries of brick and concrete rose like effigies to a glory long gone from the world, empty of the people who day by day built up a little bit less, tore down more than they reckoned, and left themselves without the grace those yesteryears had inspired. "Everyone fucks up now and again. It's just a question of degrees."

Tina shifted uncomfortably in her seat. "I learned all this stuff in Sunday School. And you really think it's real?"

"Do you not?" I replied, offering the nicest smile I could to the girl in the mirror.

"I don't know."

"Then nothing I say will convince you whether it's real or not, Tina. The only person I can be true to is the Lord, but I'm being true to you, too. There it is."

"That's intense, Patrick."

"So are exorcisms."

We crossed the bridge before dawn broke the skyline, its length blued by the coming light. Brooklyn washed awake on the other side in shades of navy darkened against the orange-gold, clinging to the last bits of stained shadows while windows flashed at the sun's emergence. The bridge went on like something in a pop-modern painting, steel striped in beams of brightness. Closer to my final destination, that nagging in my shoulders and neck subsided.

I'd be able to sleep soon.

"So, if there are demons, then there are definitely angels," she said, more to herself than me, I reckoned. "Do angels possess people?"

"Never met one."

"You exorcise demons and you don't know if there are angels?"

"All I said was that I've never met an angel," I repeated. Best way to tend the flock was to take them outside of the fence. The ones that didn't want to know stayed in, but the others that followed the shepherd never returned—or some pseudo-spiritual nonsense I applied to this situation. "But the rules are the same. They live in Heaven and come to us in the heart and mind, never in the flesh. At least not like they used to."

"Like demons."

"Right. But no horns, Tina, and certainly no wings."

"So, are you here to rid someone of a demon?"

"I actually banished one before you picked me up."

She stared right at me in the rearview, paying no attention to Brooklyn's empty side streets. "You're fucking with me."

"I'm true to you, Tina," I replied as I checked the GPS again. A mile and a few minutes to go. "You and the Lord."

I almost expected her to end the ride then and there, either exasperated by this mouthy Irish weirdo taking the piss out of her or out of the pure terror of having to share her swanky Corolla with a bona fide crazy person.

Thank God she didn't ask about the reincarnation-slash-transcendence bit.

Tina drove on, silent, until the last turn down a street in Bushwick along a row of old shops renewed through recent renovation. Rich whites who had moved in and moved the poor out had repainted the buildings in garish colors, somewhere between multicolor acid vomit and Dada. Where trash and homeless once reigned, only the latter remained, living monuments to apathy in the world's sparkling metropolis.

Twain would have had something to say if he was alive. Probably something quotable but obvious.

Then Tina surprised me. "Do you help them, at least?"

"Excuse me?" I asked.

"The demons," she said. "Do they ever get forgiven?"

Those not in the know surprised me sometimes. "All I know is that when I'm done, the person who was possessed isn't anymore. To see them free is sometimes good enough."

She cocked a dark eyebrow. "Sometimes?"

"You're too smart, aye, Tina?" I said, prickled by the question, though I hid it behind another bit of practiced friendliness. This one got to me.

We pulled up to my destination in Williamsburg. African statues of animals and Lwas cluttered the windows of a lone brownstone wedged between a swanky new wine shop that wasn't there last time and a boutique with the latest teen-wear for adults. The statues' garish faces snarled at the coming morning. A collapsed placard bore the painted symbols of a purple eye next to some Tarot cards, which always drew a grin out of me—Merry didn't know shit about Tarot.

I unbuckled my seat belt. Tina and I shared one last look.

"Are you for real, Patrick?" she asked a second time.

"You know what I'll say. Thanks for the ride and God bless."

She rolled down the passenger window when the car door shut.

"Hey, Patrick," she called after me, her thick New York accent shining through.

"Aye, Tina?"

"Where are you going?"

Her big brown eyes stared right into me, and for a moment, I considered telling her that I was figuring out a place for her to park so we could go get coffee. Every bit of every day of this life growing up in that monastery, surrounded by the same boring assholes for eighteen years, shouted meager warnings for me not to do it, to move on, to get back to my point on this rock.

Refuse my sins.

The ministry had nothing on that girl's face.

I thumbed over my shoulder. "Just into this Voodoo temple, love. God bless and be safe."

3

WALL OF LWAS

D id you really think this would be enough, Tater?" Mama Merry inquired, a frown on her pretty face.

I look down at our stash between us in disappointment. I had brought an ounce and already smoked more than half. "You knew my predilections when you invited me."

She sat up on the ratty old red couch, bead bracelets rattling as she gesticulated at me with those long hands. "You're supposed to be a saint, you shit-ass." She dropped back down to her side of the cushions, followed by a brief glower before the pout ended. She shrugged her dark shoulders, pinching a bit of mossy magic and stuffing it into the rainbow glass spoon we had shared over the last few hours. Falling back onto me, she nestled her head into the crook of my shoulder, shifting beneath our shared sheet. Red silk on her toned body slithered against my flesh while she searched for the lighter.

I traced my fingers along her bare shoulder. "Don't take it all."

She pulled a few puffs and exhaled the French way, out the mouth and into her nose. "After that performance, you should be a bit more charitable. You priests are supposed to be scions of charity, right?"

I let Merry kiss me after she gave me the pipe, her breath earthen and ash with hints of the honeydew we'd eaten downstairs. Fucked up, but it was better than my first life in Ireland, where suffering, serpents, and souls was the taste of the dew. Lots of lost souls. But I also was a priest before the Church had that silly Lateran-thing. Celibacy was for the birds. This Vodun priestess and I had been going on and off for years after the Vatican sent me to Haiti to handle the things their regular exorcists couldn't.

She and I deemed the relationship our "ecumenical deal" after our first scuffle, and we had been together since. No strings, no apologies, and no commitments when apart—only with each other when God afforded us the time.

It was the closest thing we allowed to love.

We lay there while the sun wound its light through the windows at the front of the brownstone, the CLOSED sign a shield between us and the world.

"This was a nice surprise," she said in her sleepy accent. Her hand snaked across my tattooed chest.

"I guess I should keep it nice." I pressed my lips to her smooth forehead.

Merry sighed against my mouth. "What are you here for?"

"I wanted to keep it nice."

She glared at me with the barest hint of a smile, those amber eyes filling my vision.

I broke under those gems. "I need to speak to them." I nodded at the statues clustered in the corners of the queen's bedroom, often the only other witnesses to our agreements.

"Oh," she said, relieved at what seemed a simple request. "You could have just called me from Rome."

"That would have set off a firestorm." They tracked my phones since the day they handed me the first. They probably knew I was here now, in the home of a heretic and 'evildoer.' I lay back against the corduroy pillow, the ridges irritating my neck. "Probably setting off a firestorm now."

Merry bounded off the bed like a red deer, her lithe form dancing around the room in movements of perfect muscle and curves in the right places. She wrapped herself in a gorgeous length of pink-gold silk patterned in West African motifs and gathered her long braids up into one massive bun, a vision of Erzulie herself.

"Get up out of bed," she ordered, walking back to yank the sheets off.

A sudden chill attacked my wetted parts, forcing me into a curl. "Can I at least have a shower?" I crowed, trying my best to maintain what little modesty the Lord ever afforded me in the first place.

"No," she said, walking toward the doorway out to the hall, silks trailing behind her like a grand train. "The lwas will like us this way."

"Oh, of course they will." I sat up on the edge of the bed, grabbing one of the denim belt loops on my jeans with my big toe. Pulling them to my hand, I slid the dark wash onto my skinny legs. Barefoot and shirtless, I plodded out to the hall to follow her down the bisected passage to the other bedroom on the brownstone's second floor.

Merry had already lit the candles by the time I ambled in, the warm glow revealing a ritual space.

Her altar, a small block of rectangular wood from her native Haiti that once served as a column-piece in a great temple to Ogun, lay littered in a collection of half-used incense cones, melted wax, and bowls of herbs, jewels, candies, cigarettes, and more that fought for space beside old statues stained dark in smatters of blood, honey, and whatever else crusted them. In the farthest left corner stood a blue vase filled with dying flowers, soft in their decay.

But the altar drew little of my attention compared to what it sat in front of.

Painted the brightest color of robin's egg blue, the smoothed bricks of the wall looked out upon the room and its occupants. I had seen the Wall of the Lwas so many times, I realized, but every time I saw it again, it frightened me. Old gods resided there, and for all my faith in the Lord Almighty, I didn't deny these in the middle of their realm.

Merry brought a cup of cold chicken blood out of a small fridge in the corner. Motioning me to sit dead center on the floor atop a painted sigil to Erzulie Danto, she started her work. A particularly coarse aspect of the priestess' goddess, I always viewed her a bit like Mary—best friend to those she likes, and hell to those otherwise.

She answered when I needed her, at least.

Merry bent down in front of me, dipping her fingers into the open container of blood. "This will be gross."

There was a part of me that wondered what I was doing as she started drawing veves on my chest, shoulders, and back, before lining my face in dashes of red. My side of the spiritual party believed taking part in magic and ritual opened one's soul to the foes of Heaven and Earth, allowing the entrance of demons that created the need for those like me. My ministry came before all that medieval bullshit, so I didn't know either way, only what I had seen.

Still, I prayed.

Are you there?

Our father, who art in Heaven, hallowed be thy name...

Her work finished, Merry took a bowl of yellow powder from her altar, a concoction of herbs that would put me under until the calling ended. Grabbing a handful of the talc-like stuff, she looked me in the eye and grinned, that smile I knew so well hemmed with sincere worry. God wanted us to know things, we of faith all agreed, but when and where was His business, and if He thought it best to say no, then I would find out the hard way the moment that powder hit my nostrils.

Thy Kingdom Come, thy will be done,

On earth as it is in Heaven,

And giving your daily bread,

Forgive me for my sins,

As I forgive those who sinned.

Lead me not to temptation but deliver me from evil.

For thine is the kingdom, and the power, and the glory...

Merry smothered my face with a handful of her magic dust.

The transition from this world to the place between came softly through my skull, which would have been worse if I wasn't higher than a giraffe's asshole. The sear of neurons kicking off chemical loads climbed up the front of my face.

Merry chanted. Low, long, her voice echoed past me and within.

The pain subsided, but the heat in my head remained, boiling gray matter until the world wrinkled.

In the distance, bells and drums clattered while Merry's voice threaded in my eyes to wrap around my mind. Like her pink-gold silk, I felt my body swaddled in a warm, smooth blanket of pressure. My stomach, empty save for the few shots of whiskey she and I shared earlier alongside our fruit, gurgled in protest of the hallucinogen.

Time warped.

Colors exploded while every texture wriggled, dancing in their confinement of lines to break free and ooze into the world. Chanting echoed from the hallway outside the cracked door of the room, and the light spilling past slithered in the air like serpents before they touched the old, polished hardwoods, each board a waterfall of lacquer and grains.

Merry danced around me, a goddess embodied. Her song penetrated my atoms.

I stared ahead at the blue wall, waiting for the real show to start.

The paint crawled before my eyes like roaches, a thousand tesseracts folding in on themselves endlessly until, without warning, dozens of faces lifted from the surface. The roaring face of Ogun, Erzulie's blazing eyes, and Legbas' endless snicker filled my ears.

"I hear you, Saint Patrick," a woman's voice echoed in the depths of my soul. I shuddered, knowing I had come to the feet of Love's lwa. "Oh, I hear you so well."

"At least you speak back," I warbled in the myriad dimensions.

She laughed, deep and husky. "You've always been an odd one. Getting on with old gods, failing your own scriptures..."

Legbas uttered something I couldn't understand in old Creole and a mish-mash of things that sound like West African dialects, but I was too balls-to-the-walls high to know. The lwas chatted to each other while I reeled. My guts threatened to betray me.

"I followed the ones that were contemporary to my time. Big difference." A flare of light spiked the center of my brain, a harsh rebuke to my arrogance. Somehow my body stayed up, beyond my will. I swallowed burning bile once or twice. "And I don't follow them anymore."

"Careful," Erzulie whispered. "I help those that are sweet."

I fixed my eyes on the blue wall, thinking I spotted her face at the corner of a brick. "I didn't come to your gaff to insult you."

"Better," said Erzulie. "So you're here for her?"

"Her?"

"Don't be coy, Irish."

"I'm not," I said, my voice many miles away from where I sat. "Where is she? Who is she? Why did that demon want me to find her?"

"Questions aren't free, Saint Patrick," the lwas replied in unison, infusing incense and song.

Merry gyrated with her rattles and bells, whipped into a passion of blood and ecstasy. She licked her lips at me when she caught my attention off to the side, her eyes alight with the infernos of the ancient world. Her shift flared out as she went, revealing the perfection of black skin and curves cut from years of marching this world to see the spirits made true.

And yet, something differed this time. Not aroused, nor enchanted, a gloom fell on me.

I had never felt more disconnected from her than in that moment.

I knew, then and there, this would be the last time we were what we were. The terror of it flooded my heart, and for a moment, I thought of saying nothing, of letting the ritual carry on until my priestess tired or the lwas grew bored of me.

"What will this cost me?" I asked them, still riding around the pocks in the paint like merry-go-rounds.

"Oh, you just told yourself that." Erzulie's coy laughter nearly shook me apart.

The blue wall distended out toward me, as if made of blue raspberry Jell-o instead of concrete. Whatever the fuck it was, I didn't know. Images of dancing, killing, reveling spirits directed by the greatest soul played out their displays of power and grandeur. I watched Ogun slaughter hundreds before his wife spoke again.

"She's here," Erzulie Danto whispered to me.

"In America?" I asked, unable to put those words in the longer sentence I wanted.

"Try the next borough, you lazy-ass." The smell of burning tobacco filled my nose while rum burnt my tongue. "Now, Saint Patrick, wake up. And may your god bless you, for you shall have need of it."

The old gods of West Africa cackled in my ears, always knowing more they wouldn't tell.

4

THE FIRST PHONE CALL

She waited by the front door, holding her silk in front of her body. Merry and I passed the last joint she had rolled, saying little as we hazed the space between us. For the oven my brain and body had endured, she looked far worse for wear than I did, having poured body and soul into the ritual. Her skin had taken on a gray pallor, the effect of effort and powers meeting.

"Who do you think she is?" she asked.

I handed her the joint and wiped the residue on my hand on the side of my jeans. "Fuck if I know. My guess is that some Satanists kidnapped some poor girl thinking they'll bring about the end of the world."

Merry grunted, smoke bobbing from her mouth as she spoke. "I hear those don't involve chickens."

"Just rape and murder."

The cab I had called ten minutes ago pulled up outside, its light illuminating Brooklyn's foggy night. Safe in the priestess' warm, welcoming house, I gazed past the glass at the chariot to my next doom.

"You goin'?"

My eyes fell on my lover, my friend, and for a second I thought about breaking the promise made between a priestess and her patient: what happened to me happened to me, and that was a blessing to keep to myself. Or was it? Knowing this would be the last time we made love, danced with each other alone, or even held hands as something more than friends...

I turned my attention to the cab outside. "Yeah, I'm going."

Our embrace lasted longer, at least on my end. This silent goodbye stung hard, harder than I imagined. I broke away from Merry and she let me out into the world.

The cabbie's window was blessedly shut, giving me time alone when he pulled away to drive south down as many streets as I paid him for, toward Bed-Stuey.

My phone vibrated in the pocket of my jeans. I fished it out and looked at the screen.

The Chair.

I had missed sixty calls he had made, ignored twenty-two texts, and five voicemails I was sure would be neither fun nor pleasant to listen to if I cared.

I tapped my thumb on the screen's little green button and put the phone to my ear. "How weighs the miter, Frank?"

"Where are you?" asked the voice on the other end, a very serious Argentinian man.

"You know bloody well where I am. You've tracked this phone since the moment I lifted off in Italy."

"What are you doing, Saint Patrick? This is against every protocol we have for the March. The college of exorcists has even moved to strip you of your license and resources."

"Let them. None of us work for you anyway. You'll do nothing."

Silence held the other end for a moment, followed by a deep, despairing sigh. "Patrick, please. The Church is praying for you. We are concerned."

"About what?" I asked. "About what? About the three hundred demons I've successfully exorcised? About what? About the years you put me and the other children through hell so you would have your little army against Satan? Tell me, father—what do you pray for me over?"

His answer came with an edge to it, though give the man credit—out of all those red-caped bastards, his white one was deserved. "We are, of course, blessed by all things you and the saints do for us. God has given the world great providence, but you have spent hours in the company of a heretic! A Vodun priestess, no less!"

"Oh, fuck you lot." I noticed the driver staring at me through his rearview mirror. I gave him the finger, which made him look away. "That 'heretic' does more to save lives in New York and heal the sick than our priests do these days when they aren't secretly buggering everything that moves. Don't you sit there, on that chair, and tell me that a devout priestess devoted to her community and child molesters are the same thing."

"Your ecumenical views are yours, Patrick, and you know I've taken a hard stance to make the Church more open to the fullness of God's creations, but she's a heathen. She cavorts with spirits and demons."

"So did I and so did Christ. Not every person that deserves saint-hood need die for the Cross."

The Chair gasped at my sacrilege. "You cannot repeat that again. Not to me and not in front of the clergy."

"Oh, am I on speaker? I was here earlier than you were, Father, and the rest of you. I'll err on the side of goodness over dogma as Christ did in the temple."

"You'd call us money changers now?" The poor man, who was a good, kind, gentle man who never did me wrong, asked the question like I had struck him. Fairness to him, he came from one of those poor countries where the Church did do some good. They turned out a damned fine mind and a good, honest soul to lead the Vatican.

But he still didn't lead me. "Aren't you?"

"We're sending someone to come find you," said the Chair, short and to the point. "Please do not be difficult. We are only here to serve and help you, Saint Patrick, but only if you let us."

"You'll do nothing."

I ended the call as the front grill of a black SUV slammed into the side of the taxi.

The cabbie screamed something in Farsi as our backend fishtailed hard into a telephone pole, twisting it in a new trajectory onto the sidewalk. Bowled on my side, my seat belt held me to the bench as the Lincoln smashed into a stoop. Clawing at the buckle, I kicked at my door as smoke filled the cabin.

The heels of my Docs shattered the window, letting out enough to thin the cloud. I tore at the strap pinning my waist, ripping it out with a jerk. Crawling for the door handle, I pulled, the electric locks still functioning enough to flick upward. Tumbling out of the totaled vehicle, I fought to gain my bearings as the world spun.

I heard the cabbie kick open the door on the other side, cursing as he dug his foot out of the broken plastic. He stood up and dropped to his knees, clutching his neck and shoulder.

Rolling forward to my feet, I held onto the cab and started to limp around the back. "Hey! Hey," I shouted, my balance faulty.

He lay on his side, groaning loudly about his neck while orange flames burst from the vents on the smoking dash. I forced myself steady, snorting as I bent over. I almost jostled him when I noticed a figure approaching in the distance.

Tall and handsome, his dark brown hair swooped right against a small part, the sides and back faded to the skin. His bright blue eyes locked with mine, those pools inhabited with clear, violent conviction.

He carried a medieval broadsword in his right hand.

I couldn't hear the footfalls of his boots over the sound of the burning cab behind me, but I knew the bastard well enough.

Saint George of England, the Dragonslayer, had come to claim his Irish compatriot on behalf of the Vatican.

It was always the fucking English.

5

BLOODY BRITISH

We stood facing each other with the burning cab to our side, blinking through the smoke to keep stock of whoever made the first move. George's sword seemed to float in his grip.

Never one for weapons, I lifted my hands in the pose of peace. Thunder broke the sky.

"Was that the only phone call I get, sheriff?" I asked the knight.

"Stand down, Patrick," he said in that ever-so-slight-but-forever-present tone of condescension I knew so well. Maybe it was because I was Irish but fucking poshes like George always put on airs. "You're lucky that the order doesn't involve killing you."

"Because the Lord loves the idea of his saints murdering each other." I stuck my hands into the pockets of my coat. Tangling my fingers in the greenstone beads of my rosary, I close my right on the spine of my small Bible. Not a great shield against a steel blade, but I had worse in the past. "We're doing this?"

George opened his shaved gob, the fool. "We wi—"

I walked right into the Englishman's face, caring nothing for his sword or his pompous Italian boots, one of which I kicked with the front of mine. "What are you going to do?"

"We're not boys anymore, Patrick." George didn't flinch. "You don't have your little clique to come fight your battles."

"Oh, is the poor little Englishman finally getting to have his hero moment? Finally find something you can do that won't result in a charge?"

His eyes narrowed, teeth gritted. He stepped back and raised his blade at me, the point at my chest. "You're coming with me, you mouthy little bastard."

"I ain't going fucking anywhere I don't want, and there ain't a fucking thing you can do about it." I scoffed at his Trafalgar fashions, the skinny jeans, the it-came-ratty sweater, the stupid little coat over a cardigan. Even his sword had gold, the prat. "Look at you! I don't know if you're coming to take me to Rome or fucking SoHo to meet your 'friend' Andre!"

George cocked his arm back to strike. "You ugly little—" He halted his blow. He stomped away for a moment, cursing something under his breath. He faced me again, the point of his weapon toward the pavement. "Get in the fucking car, Patrick, or I'll beat you into it."

"Go fuck yourself."

He swung out at me, the flat of his blade aimed for my neck.

I turn into it as I wheeled a hard roundhouse kick into his side, accepting the whipping sting across my back. The sole of my boot blew the air out of George when I caught the bottom of his ribs, knocking him back to give me room. Unable to control his body for lack of air, he dropped his sword. My next kick sent the glittering edge down the street, where it slid toward the mouth of a sewer.

We charged each other like we were boys again.

My left cross connected with his jaw, stopping him dead in his tracks. George stumbled onward, throwing his weight behind a short right that pressed my nose to my cheek. Confident he hadn't broken my face, I backstepped and threw into another hard cross to his mush. That one dropped him to a knee, but stiff upper lip and all that. George roared like a lion into a tackle, planting me hard to the concrete.

The Church taught us how to kill each other.

From the moment they found one of us—saints reborn—we were taken from our families and placed in a single monastery so far in remote Italy you truly saw the ravages of God and the Devil. The man atop of me had nightmares of legendary dragons—dragons—and the same terror that fueled his rage pounded his fists into my forearms.

Too wild, too angry, I let him wear himself out on my guard while bringing my feet to his stomach. He over swung, allowing me the angle needed to pitch him off balance.

George rolled to his feet at the same time I did, his hair doused from a murky puddle that turned his face sourer than it had been before. Blood dripped from his nose, matching my own.

I heaved. A clot in my nostrils forced me to breathe through my mouth. "Come on, you bastard. Come on."

"I've always fucking hated you," he said at me, spitting out a red glob. "I fucking hate you!"

My laughter made him charge forward into a shovel left that planted George flat on his back. I reared back my broken hand, ready to tag him another when a flash of lightning revealed that his eyes had rolled back into his head.

A sudden wheeze gathered a knot of blood and snot in my chest, halting my surprise in a hacking cough. I bent over again and vomited the ball of yellow-red goodness.

My adrenaline dump ended when an elevating pain flushed throughout my battered body, and the burning cab's smoke made my eyes sting. The lights of George's battered SUV flooded in, causing my knees to wobble. An urge to vomit a second time boiled in my throat before better sense took me. Looking down at George one more time, I pulled out my phone and tossed it on his stomach.

No more bullshit from Rome.

My journey through Brooklyn's network of alleyways and cross streets gave me time to take stock on the way to Bedford, where I knew I could find a park or two to hide in. Checking for my Bible, vestment, rosary, crucifix, keys to the apartment in Dublin, I found my wallet in the back pocket of my jeans. Three hundred dollars US and a black card, with some pounds in change.

Shit. Shit, shit, shit, shit, shit.

I ditched the black card in a dumpster before I decided on a subway station instead of hoofing it on foot. Disappearing down the steps into the bowels of New York, I spent my first twenty on a Metro Pass. I bought it from a booth next to a homeless man. I blessed him and donated the second twenty because I kind of had to.

I blew a good hundred on a burner from a twenty-four-hour shop at some station. "Fuck. Fuck," I whispered, mashing numbers as I jogged up the steps. There was a good signal in Midwood.

A few tries and a few blocks later, Merry picked up. "Hello?"

"Don't stay on the line too long, lass."

"Patrick?"

The city at night surged around me, too many sights and sounds to track and too little time to calm down. Cabs whizzed past, their low beams giving me a headache. "They came after me, Merry. They sent George after me."

"My god," she said, drawn to a whisper on the other end. "Where are you?"

"Still in Brooklyn."

"Patrick, I checked with a few of my friends," she said. "My friend, Sheila—she's a Wiccan—she said that the possessed are known to gather at this joint called Bar Rochelle. You might want to look for your girl there."

"Thanks, Merry. You lock the door, alright?"

"Of course, Tater. Call me if you need me to come get you."

I smiled at the burner, at ease for a moment. "Ta." And like that, the ease left, assumed again by the stifling panic screwed in the center of my chest. I blended back into the flow of drunks and party-goers still out past midnight before I doubled back and went the other way on foot, north along Ocean Parkway.

The cold night made me shiver, worse so because of my ruined clothes. A quick walk down one of the main streets by another station, a bar named Lucky's caught my attention. The old white sign, yellowed from the years, bore God's blessing to my eyes:

"20 oz. Guinness for $3."

Fuck Rome. They wouldn't murder me sober.

The bar lay empty save for a girl behind the counter, one of those neon-haired bubblegum goths that took one look at my rumpled clothes and kept the chit-chat short.

The first glass of Arthur's drained in seconds, followed by a second and a shot of Tullamore to get my blood going. Steadied on, I sat there at the vinyl and simply stared at my draining glass, finally finding some warmth after the third or fourth round. By the time Gracie—I thought that was her name—went for the bill, I dodged out with enough cash left behind to cover it, back into the darkness before she spotted me.

Right as rain, I stopped in a little phone shop and bought a better SIM card, spending most of my remaining cash on a newer model that gave me a few gigs of data to play with. After entering Merry's number in the contacts, I got online and found the address for Bar Rochelle.

6

SESSION TWO

The tang of whiskey lingered on my tongue when I walked to Bar Rochelle, one of the new hip bars built beneath gaffs only preppy white kids could afford on their parents' money. This one Bay Ridge den in particular had all the dead give-aways of a demon's wannabe Hell, which basically amounted to a glittery Russian shithole, but without the Russians to make it fun.

Atop the doorway of the black marble façade, the establishment's name glowed Vader red in the waxing night, though the line to the entrance stretched around the building and to the curb.

The backstreet offered a way into the clean kitchen where the waitstaff hustled back and forth trays of catered snacks and whatever else Americans ruined their stomachs with at the pub. Barbacks broke open bottles of overpriced Cristal while the keeps hocked their wells, wetting the red tiles behind the bar until a sudsy puddle grew. Steaming platters of crab-stuffed egg rolls wafted next to soggy mushrooms crusted with parmesan under heat lamps set too close.

I stole a few of the fungi on the way through the galley between the kitchen and club, gaining not a lick of attention. For all the staff knew, I was probably a dealer or someone too important to walk in through the front and simply not worth the hassle. The smell of the dance floor itself, spilled beer and too much perfume mixed with sweaty cologne, washed over me as I entered the club's main room, where the glass walls vibrated to the electro-beat.

Bar Rochelle popped off as 50 Cent rumbled the speakers. Honeys wearing short neon skirts and spilling out of their tops danced atop bars for the happy patrons, drunken louts too gone to notice the bouncers circling the room, on the hunt for the first person that drew their ire.

The friars who had raised me never understood how I had been able to sneak from their care, especially on the festival days when they took us to the village to celebrate this holiday or that holiday. For all the talk about not being pagans, we certainly celebrated like them. I could still hear the lambs bleating before they were bolted in the head and stripped of their flesh. God brought people together in the weirdest ways.

I held no great secret to do it, as I did it the same way they did it within the Mossad—act like you're supposed to be there. I headed around the crowds of screaming bachelorettes and hipster bros and found an empty spot at the counter.

The bartender finally noticed me after three minutes of her looking me dead in the eye and ignoring any attempt to serve me. She didn't even greet me when she neared.

"There a quiet place in here?" I shouted at her over the music.

The bartender, with pins of sharp steel sprouting from her brow in a complete line along the ridge, rolled her eyes at me and pointed to a roped-off area in the back, leading to a terrace where patrons could watch what went on, sniff some coke, while still having a good shot at the bathrooms before lines formed. I walked away without thanking her and her hardware-glare.

Demons were voyeurs by nature of their incorporeal state, which made discovering them hard to discern until it was too late and their hosts clawed chunks from the walls. But those were the dumb ones.

There were many, many smart demons, and the process they perfected after they latched upon a simple soul remained simple: pull the host toward a bad decision here, raise an unworthy urge there, and usher the person they commanded along the path to Perdition in small ways. Sometimes taking years before the poor victim's body succumbed to a malady that every doctor and scientist deemed mental illness later, many normal exorcists often found them too late to do anything about it.

God didn't like that business, hence we saints. We had a keen sense for them, almost a radar.

They were in the back, sitting together on three red couches that faced each other. The circular table between them lay scattered with razor blades, empty liquor bottles, messy smears of white powder beside rolled twenties. Twelve in total, they ceased their conversation when they noticed me across the room. Silent, they waited, their angry eyes promising violation.

I offered a friendly wave when I approached. "Hi, all," I said, pulling my Bible from my coat pocket. "Any of you heard the Good Word?"

"You think we don't know who you are?" one of them asked, a blonde near the center of the pack. Even in the dimness of the club, her eyes shone onyx, the whites eaten away by evil. The rest of them didn't move a single muscle, as if they didn't breathe.

"We're all fans, by the way," she continued.

"Excuse me?" I asked.

Uh oh. These were the smart ones.

"We enjoy your work, Saint Patrick," The Blonde said.

A few of the demons matched her smile, too perfectly in sync. The minute detail of it raised a terror within me. Breathing through my teeth and nose as I smiled, I kept my tone even as possible. "Well," I said, holding up my Bible for them to see me shut it with a clap. "It's nice to have admirers."

"Did you truly make Satan drop his meal once?" one of the demons asked, a young man I'd swear was twelve if not for his garish fashion choices.

"Aye, lad, right where Cashel Rock sits." Okay, it was nice to have actual fans. I stuck the Good Book back into its proper pocket. I wouldn't need it anyway. "So let's get to business, because as much as I love you all, we both know that I'm not here to sign autographs and let you buy me shots."

"You're here for her," said the Blonde.

"Okay, stop," I said, my hands up. Scanning their faces, I suddenly got what the problem was. "Oh, you're all the underlings."

A few of the demons possessed of varying sizes of strong men stood up.

I hopped on the low table cornering two of the couches together, arms out like the Savior. "What? What the fuck will you do?"

"What the fuck will you do?" the Blonde asked, too calm for her own good as she remained seated across the coffee table from me.

"There are more of us than there are of you, Saint Patrick," added the twelve-year-old. Deep in the confines of his Misfits hoodie, his face contorted into something inhuman, ridges and spikes riding beneath flesh. Light glistened on his teeth, gums blackened by poison.

Illusions, and amateur ones at that.

I laughed in their faces. "Oh, okay. Let me tell you how this works." Pulling out the last few wads of cash crushed in my coat pocket, my lighter comes out as well. "See this money? I don't give a fuck about this money. Just God's work. Ah, sprinklers! These ceilings are set to go off at the first sign of fire. I can make a fire, I tell you what!"

A few of them hesitated, shifting for the first time in their seats.

"Imagine it." I clicked my fingers. "A quick blessing and this becomes the holiest sprinkler party ever."

"We'll kill you before you utter a word," the Blonde replied.

"You'll do nothing," I said back, hiding my absolute terror behind a smirk.

I desperately didn't want to fight all of them. I flat couldn't.

All twelve of them, even the ones standing, took a moment to measure me.

They were dead right. I was done the moment they made a move, but that anger made even the cunning falter. Smart as they were, these demons were also young, most likely Lucifer's bottom tier of angels that got the short end when they fell. After George, the wreck, part of me broke at the thought.

Everyone suffered in the tug of war between Heaven and Hell.

Even these demons.

But why did I give a damn?

"There's too many people here," the twelve-year-old said aloud.

"And here I thought your lot would love to be on YouTube," I replied before any of his friends did.

The Blonde stared daggers at me, which I'm sure she would have yanked from her own eyes to stab me with. She broke her focus, looking at the table between us. "She's downstairs in the basement."

The twelve-year-old protested. "Mehmet!"

Never mind, they were idiots. All I ever needed was their names and God would make them do the rest. What happened if they ever possessed someone and I came calling?

Ugh, youths.

"Quiet, Nariel," the Blonde snapped back, literally forcing me to keep my mouth closed. "We're ordered to let him find her. Murdering him and everyone in this club won't do us any favors. Or let us come back."

Uh oh.

"But this fucking potato-eater!" cried the twelve-year-old.

"It doesn't matter," she said, rising to her feet.

The rest still seated rose with her in a perfect harmony of movement. On a silent order, the demons filed out of the back area, leaving behind mounds of trash and half-drunk vodka bottles. Mehmet remained, her stare fixed upon me until we were the only ones.

"We really are fans," she said, taking a pair of padlock keys out of the impossibly-tight pockets of her impossibly-tight jeans and tossing them on the table.

"Why?" I asked, unable to hide my surprise. Nothing in the world should have been this easy.

"It is always good to appreciate one's enemy."

She left, and alone in the private seating area of the club, I never felt more exposed.

The club's thump had left my skull by the time I threaded through the kitchen on the way back to the alley again, finding the building's access hatch for the basement beside the overflowing dumpsters. It opened to a musty darkness, wet and rot from the puddled floors where the foundations of Bar Rochelle had cracked. I used the flashlight on my burner to lead my way down the steps.

The basement stretched long into oblivion, the bass of the speakers vibrating the ceiling as I walked deeper. Dust fell on my head and shoulders. The pulsing beat increased until it nearly deafened me, forcing me into a hunch as I covered both ears. A touch of the phone to my head turned off the flash. Left to darkness, the pitch basement offered no path, no way, and no hope to wherever God had sent me.

Then I saw a light.

The outline of some crates against a far wall cut angles in the dark. Stumbling forward, I opened my Bible and ripped the last few pages out, the blank ones scrawled with some old notes. Twisting them into ropes while keeping my phone in one hand, I rolled the paper into wads and stuffed them in my ears. The pounding subsided, allowing me the peace to pick my way toward the illumination.

Rounding the crates, I literally dropped my phone, unable to hold on to it.

Not that I needed the flashlight.

The long wings glowed like weregold, each feather smoother than silk. They folded around the naked body of a young woman, fluttering in perfect movement every time she breathed.

Her golden eyes peeked out at me from behind them.

An angel peeked at me.

7

DEEVI

I shoved open the hatch to the street, turning and offering my
hand. The angel followed without protest, though the confused
expression on her face to the world outside could not have been
any clearer. Holding my peacoat in front of her to cover her exposed
body, I left her in the alley and ran out to the sidewalk.

People filtered in and out beneath Bar Rochelle's hellish neons.

A few minutes later I returned, searching through the clutch some
tart had left on the curb as her and her drunk friends piled into a
limo. iPhone, lipsticks, a wad of hundreds, a vial of coke, and a small
fold with five different pieces of plastic made the sin worth it.

"Hurry," I whispered to the angel, offering my hand again.

She looked at me once with her golden eyes before moving, her
flawless feet soft upon the grimy concrete. The fresh smell of the rain
could not hide the odor of the kitchens when we passed, the burnt
grease and roasted potatoes drawing her toward the door. I directed
her away, toward the other end of the alley, where I called an Uber
while we hid for a few minutes.

Taking time to make sure the coat covered her naked body in the
cold night, I brushed her damp, dark hair from her eyes while trying

to figure out what the fuck I was going to do with an angel in New-Goddamn-Fucking-York. "Okay, we're going to get a ride, yeah? Quick ride to some place warm."

The angel smiled at me. "That would be nice."

"You speak?"

She simply smiled back at me, hiding something behind it.

The Uber pulled up, a carrier van meant for eight that I prayed God had let some kind Japanese designer with the insight to accommodate appendages for flight. Unable to process that I had just spoken to an actual angel on Earth, I motioned for her to stay put once more and walked as calmly as I could to the curb.

The driver, an Algerian, lowered the window of his gray van and smiled. "Hi, are you Patrick?"

"That's me, bud," I said. "Look, I'm a photographer with Victoria's Secret, and I need to get my model to the Mark on 77th on the East Side of Manhattan for the next shoot. You know it?"

The nice man, with his balding head and bushy mustache, leaned forward in the driver's seat to look at the angel. "Is she wearing wings?"

"Yeah, big ones," I said, trying to keep my cool.

His smile diminished. "Let me put down the backseat."

I ushered the angel into the back of the van. We shared the bench as comfortably as possible, crowded by the extra mass of her wings, which brought us close together as the gray avenues and empty streets flashed by in the predawn hours.

"You speak English," I said to her, whispering so the driver could not hear us. Between the noise of his radio station and his lackluster gaze out the windshield, we were left alone.

"I speak all tongues," she said, staring me dead in the eyes. Wonder played in her gaze until she broke from me, a small, sincere smile forming as we neared the Brooklyn Bridge. Steel and wire and road, the behemoth of human achievement towered, its signal lights bright white against the burnt night sky.

"Oh." God stuff. Heard it before. "Do you have a name?"

She said nothing, too mesmerized by the bridge.

We arrived at the Mark Hotel on the east side of Central Park, down from the Met. I checked us in with straight cash and left the angel in a room on the tenth floor before hitting Duane Reade down the street, where I got her some sweats, underwear, and toiletries. A bottle of Green Spot from the liquor store across the way, where I pulled out as much money from the first credit card as I could before I ditched it in a trashcan, allowed time for a breath and taste of peace before I visited a few more stores, unloading the rest for as much cash as I could before ridding myself of them in the hotel's lobby bathroom.

I had my first panic attack sitting in one of the stalls trying to collect myself.

Demons were not able to walk the earth.

Neither were angels.

What the fuck was I supposed to do with an angel? Why had a demon sent me to find her?

I took hold of that panic standing before the white door to the room on the Mark's tenth floor, the hallway dead silent. She was watching TV when I came in, her body curled around a pillow as she held out the remote, clicking through the channels. Her wings were flopped over the other side of the bed. For a moment, she looked like a real Victoria's Secret model lying there, trying to zone out after a long day of doing whatever Victoria's Secret models did.

It didn't help that she was a brunette, either.

I sat on the other bed with my bags from Reade. "What are you watching?"

"Everything."

More God stuff. "Think you might be telling me your name now?"

The angel sat up on the bed, causing me to turn away when I realized I stared at her body too long.

The stir in my groin made me grit my teeth. Why did I feel shamed? The news on the box caught my attention, blaring images of missile slamming into the homes of far-off innocents while politicians played Monopoly with human lives and human hearts, harming God's creation while they changed money with the spiritual leaders they bought with washed cash.

The Church took part in that too.

"Who are you?" she asked, her gaze breaking from the TV-screen.

Drawn by the question, an immediate urge overtook me. I felt this need, this pull, to answer in full, to let her know the very depths of my heart and mind and soul, everything to satisfy the question. My panic returned like a bolt of lightning. "My name's Patrick. I was sent to rescue you by a demon I exorcised from a young girl in Italy, then a Chinese cook. I don't know why."

Pleased for the moment, the angel went back to her news-watching.

Swallowing my sheer unease at what just happened, I opened one of the shopping bags. "I bought you some things. I didn't know your size so if we have to get something else, it'll be no problem. I can call room service in a few minutes and there's a shower you can probably—"

"You stole money from a young woman to pay for those clothes," said the angel, eyes glued to a report about bombings in Syria. "Why?"

I studied the white plastic bags in my lap, trying to find some reason beyond the simple and couldn't. "I don't know why I'm here, but the people that I worked for have given their last fuck about me, you're an impossibility, what's on my back is wet to the point of shit, and you're completely naked. I didn't know what else to do besides steal us what we needed so we can get to figuring out what the hell is going on."

"Why?" she asked, almost too pleasant for the question. "Why did you decide to do that first?"

"I've not the bloody time to beg. Not now."

The angel threw her legs over the bed's edge, her breasts on full display. She grinned at me. "My name's Deevi."

Trying not to stare directly at her wonders, I nodded with a muted smile. "Nice to meet you."

"Why won't you look at me, Patrick?"

Again, I was compelled to answer. "Because you're beautiful and naked and I'm ashamed?"

Deevi took my hand in hers. Our eyes locked, yet another unspoken urge succeeding no matter how hard the will screamed against it. "I'm not shamed by your gaze," she whispered in the purest "fuck me" tone to pass my ears.

Thank God the Swiss Guard kicked in the door at that moment.

8

THE "OH FUCK" CHAPTER

Bullets ripped through our hotel room, shattering the window overlooking the street. Deevi yanked me behind her, almost tossing me over the bed. Opening her wings, she shielded me with her body, the bullets bouncing off her back, feathers, legs, and ass, which rained down in a shower of red sparks.

"Stay here until I tell you to move," she said above the roar as masked figures in the hall pumped ammo through the walls.

"What do you mean, stay—"

Deevi clapped her hands together, a flash bang that deafened my ears. The smack issued new sparks, white and black, before she drew her palms apart. A burning sword, curved and with a golden hilt that wrapped around the wielder's hand, materialized in the space between.

An indelicate sneer formed on the angel's face when she took hold of it. She turned to face the Swiss Guard.

"Follow me." Deevi marched onward, bullets ricocheting off her chest and stomach to puncture the walls until they hung in limp tatters. I grabbed my coat from the floor and the shopping bags from the bed, which by some miracle had survived the initial spray. I followed the angel, clutching our things to my chest.

"Oh fuck, oh fuck, oh fuck," I said, a representative of God's grace and bravery.

Three masked troopers beyond the doorway held their MP5s out at Deevi, unloading round after round before they slammed in more magazines when the spent ones fell. One of the broken nine-nineteens banged off the floor in front of me with a cartoony sound, like a spit in a spittoon or whatever Bugs did when he wasn't torturing Fudd for invading his forest.

Deevi roared, more lion than a woman, and charged forward. Cleaving the first two men apart, she pinned the third to the ceiling, his body sizzling on the lava-red blade. More bullets from the hallway scattered off her flesh, bounding all over and obliterating the yellow-cream wallpaper.

Blood drizzled from the Swiss Guard's stomach-hole as she yanked her weapon out of her latest victim, masking her face like Steve Austin. She strode forward. The bodies on the ground stank of shit and boiled blood, a sludgy rank steaming from the cauterized chasms her steel had opened.

I tiptoed into the hall and stopped in my tracks. "Oh, fuck."

Deevi laid open men where she walked, throwing out quick cuts that left guardsmen headless, or standing there in awed agony as their guts skirted their knees. Those that backed toward the elevators continued to fire, leaving the carpets covered in a layer of brass jackets that gleamed like Heaven's streets.

Their screams echoed in my ears for the rest of my days.

The Swiss Guard retreated by the time a dozen more bodies hit the floor, turning and running to the other end of the hallway.

I caught up to her by the elevators, having stumbled my way across a field of devastation. "Wait!"

She stopped and turned on me. "Yes, Patrick?"

"We need to leave!"

At that exact moment, the elevator doors opened. Standing in the compartment, the Swiss guardsman lifted the RPG to his shoulder, aimed for Deevi, and clicked on the trigger. The world seemed to move in slow motion, I thought, until I realized I still moved at a regular speed.

The only thing that had changed was the grenade.

Which hovered in the air, its propellant flaring blue-white.

Holding her hand out, Deevi willed the explosive to her like a damned Jedi. Golden eyes pinned to the guard who launched it, she let it float to her palm, where she held it inert.

My mouth could not have opened any wider.

"Oh, fuck," said the guardsman in Italian.

Deevi lunged forward, impaling the soldier against the back wall of the elevator. She yanked her sword out by the time I scooted inside, standing as far from the fresh corpse as I could. Her wings took up most of the room.

"Down?" she asked, the front of her body splattered in blood.

I glanced at the buttons, dumbfounded, and pressed three.

The compartment lowered, the gears above us creaking. I could hear the screams and shouts of the people on the floors we passed, and soon the smell of the guardsman's vacating bowels caused me to gag.

"What do you have in the bag?" she asked, unfazed by it all.

"Clothes," I said, nauseated as I opened my mouth to answer. "I brought you some clothes."

"Oh."

The doors parted to the third floor, and stepping out, I noticed the hall had cleared. People ran for their lives under the sounds of the massacre above them, leaving doors ajar and service carts turned over. We sneaked into one of the rooms and shut the door. Turning on the lights, I found the bathroom empty—save for a wallet and a money-clip wedged with hundreds.

"Are you a lucky charm?" I asked aloud.

"Depends on your definition of delicious."

The response made me back pedal out of the bathroom. After I made sure to slip the money into my jacket, of course. "What did you say?"

Deevi stood there, naked as the day and covered in blood like a newborn. No smile on her face, no emotion in her features, only her eyes were alight, like some sort of ravenous beast searching for something new and foreign to her.

"You need to wash off and get dressed so we can get out of here." I offered her the bag. "Here."

She looked down at it in confusion. "What am I supposed to do with that?"

For the first time, I could answer with a question. "Put them on?"

"I've never worn clothes. I won't be cold if that is what you're worried about."

Deadpan, I wiped my face with my free hand. "Please?"

"Why, Patrick?" she asked, her bloody mouth parting into a stunning smile.

Again, this urge overtook me, a need to answer her in the most honest way possible. "Because I don't want people looking at your bits as we run out of here and I'm harder than a rock. You're killing me, and if you don't put some clothes on, I'm going to need another pair of pants."

"So why don't you take them off?"

"Because then you'll see my dick," I said, unable to keep the fucking words in.

"I wouldn't mind."

Bloody, impervious, yet the very vision of everything I could ever want in a woman, she batted her long gore-crusted eyelashes, making me nearly swoon when I should not have.

"Please go get in the shower," I begged, the bags heavy in my hand.

Deevi regarded me for a moment. Not in anger or disappointment, but in a way I failed to fathom. Her burning sword, which had ebbed to a ruddy red glow, dissipated from her hand like molten bubbles popping in the air. "All right, Patrick."

"Okay."

I sat on one of the abandoned beds as she slipped into the bathroom, her wings sticking out the door. Fishing out my burner, surprise almost made me cough when I noticed a missed call on my screen.

The Chair had left a voicemail. The screen even fucking said "The Chair."

Oh, fuck. He found me on a burner.

Deevi called from the bathroom. "Patrick?"

"Yes, love?" One of these bags she left behind had my bottle of whiskey. The silken flame coated my throat in the time between our questions.

"How do you shower?"

God helped me in that moment.

"See the silver knob? Look down."

"I see it."

"Turn it to the left. Turn it back to the right a little if it gets too hot." Another shot, another spread of heat through my chest.

The water sputtered on in the bathroom.

More whiskey, more thoughtless moments. I needed the break. It was all too much at once and completely fine at the same time. The Dark Ages had been more violent, and the fact that I had walked from it unscathed... I never questioned miracles, but there in that empty bed, the heat of the potion rising, I silently wished God would stop giving me work.

The water died, and minutes later Deevi walked out. For someone who didn't understand the need for clothes, she wore a white wife-beater better than most, completed with a pair of navy sweatpants that clung too tight for my damned eyes.

I had my next uncounted sip of whiskey. "Ready?"

"Where are we going?" she asked, sticking her hands in her pockets like she was ready to head to the day's photo-shoot. The wife-beater, no matter how well she wore it, still didn't hide those wings.

Good question. I went to the window and parted the curtain. The street in front of the Mark jammed with cars. Blues and reds flashed on the wet sidewalks, clustered and separated by hundreds of people choking the ways between them when they had fled the building at the sounds of gunfire.

I wondered if the Chair called me before or after the Swiss Guard arrived.

"We need to get to my friend Merry," I said, at a loss for a better idea. "She'll help me figure out what to do."

Deevi nodded, her expression faraway.

"What?" It suddenly felt good to catch her. Thank God for whiskey. "What are you thinking?"

"I haven't thanked you yet," she said, "for rescuing me from the demons."

"T'weren't that hard." My words slurred. "Breadcrumbs every-where, if I think about it."

"Pardon?"

"No worries." The bottle got tossed into the corner. Throwing back the curtains, I unlocked the latch on the window. A quick kick popped the screen out, letting the frame fall onto the next level of the hotel's roof. A set of spotlights flicked on, and the beams floated in our direc-tion. I shut the window and stepped back, allowing the circle of light to go on by.

No stairs, no elevator. I turned on the angel. "I called you an angel."

She tilted her head to the side in confusion. "Yes?"

My attention returned to the window. Cursing under my breath for throwing away the whiskey, I opened it again. Oh fuck. The smell of the city's smoke and sour air bit my face when it rushed in. The nearest roof on the other side of the street, a hundred feet lower than from where we stood, lay empty.

"Oh, fuck," I whispered, throwing my coat on. Some quick pats to make sure the money and gear were in my pockets, I waved her in. "Fly me to that roof across the way, aye?"

Deevi snuck up behind me. "Hold tight and have faith, Patrick," she whispered in my ear. "Do you trust me?"

That urge barely toyed with me. "I don't really have a choice."

Her laughter filled my ears when she snatched me up, holding me in her arms like a rag doll. She drove through the window, her wings folded around us until she spread them upon the night air.

I opened my eyes. My first mistake.

Deevi flapped once, shooting us skyward. I involuntarily kicked my feet until they met the opposite roof.

Minutes later, when I finally found my breath again, I approached the edge of where we had landed. The chaos carried on below, roiling like a hundred snakes around stones. They had seen nothing, and all for the better.

Deevi cleared her throat. "Saint Patrick?" She waited at my back, smiling that temptress' smile. "We still have to get down."

I shut my eyes when she grabbed me for the second time. "Oh, fuck."

9

OLD GREEN YUKON

The angel and I sat on the wooden bench, watching from the small grassy lawn somewhere in Riverside Park as the eastern sky fought to keep the night from fleeing the sun. The cups of coffee we bought from a dirty cart had gone lukewarm in my hand, the dregs sludgy at the bottom.

Beside me, Deevi sat, studying her mocha before she picked it up, sniffed it, and then took a sip. A happy smile came, followed by a sensual "mmmm" before she sat the cup back down and started this process again. Even in the cold dim of the predawn, her feathers thrummed in gold light, a kind to match the sun.

I rubbed my eyes with my thumb and finger, fighting sleep and the urge to lean over and throw my arm on her shoulders, if the wings allowed it. Any thought of lechery aside, I couldn't help it. Exhausted by bullets, demons, and wanting to uncontrollably bone her for a reason beyond my understanding, I distracted myself with a more worrisome notion.

The Chair had only called once. He hadn't called again.

Unwilling to extract my phone from the breast pocket of my coat, I sipped more of my bitterness. The flat notes of the roast found my sinuses first, weak and lacking all of the excitement the hot liquid usually provided the exhausted and lonesome.

I felt so tired and alone. Cut out.

"Are you thinking on God, Patrick?"

The need to answer her question hounded me, the hackles on the back of my neck raising until the skin pinched. "Kind of always?" I responded, happy she didn't ask an easy Yes or No. The only thing worse than the stale brew was the lack of anything harder to chase it.

"You're not enjoying your delightful concoction."

"Aye, well."

She turned her head and froze me with her stare.

"Where did you come from?" I asked, the silence between us stretched too long for comfort. The glow of her wings revealed her face, a vision of beauty that could have been Irish, or Lebanese, or Indian. Whatever shape it had taken, I averted my eyes after a second, worried I'd get lost.

She repeated her ritual with the mocha. "Syria. But I was born in London."

"Really?" I played up my surprise, sitting straighter and looking about in shock. To her credit, Deevi laughed, a real laugh there on the spot, like she was some normal girl and me some fella trying to talk her into my life. I let her scoot closer. "You're not supposed to be here. I'm serious. You can't tell me that you and I both don't know."

"Know what?"

"C'mon. Demons can't take physical form. Neither can angels."

"You're the one who keeps calling me an angel."

Panic. Sheer, absolute panic. My Bible almost burned a hole in its pocket.

"Then what are you?" I asked, trying not to lean away. The possibility of it...

God didn't allow creations he did not intend. He gave permission to all things, living, dead, or otherwise.

She was impossible.

Deevi scooted closer, and before I knew what happened, her lips were upon mine. Hungry, soft, she did not grab me or push further in, but cradled me there in the moment. Dawn came in birdsong and sunlight, the dew on the grass crystalline and golden like her taste of honey and rose hips.

I broke off, leaving the bench. "I bloody can't do that."

Deevi threw up her hands in frustration. "It's not like I'd be the first woman you've mated with on a park bench!"

She nearly brought me out of my boots. I was fifteen when that happened with a girl from the nunnery next door. "How do you know about that?"

"I know everything, Patrick," Deevi said, unblinking. That earnest, endless stare—the gulf between our species—studied me in ways I never fathomed in my days of fathoming things one shouldn't. There was no fear, no uncertainty, only concern and curiosity. And need.

It made her more terrifying.

More beguiling. "Then where do you come from?"

The sun dazzled when its edge climbed the horizon, catching reds and blacks in her oaken tresses. Wind roared in the surrounding elms, the swings of a nearby playground creaking as their chains moved in the current.

"I grew up in Syria," she said. "I spent most of my life there."

A loud honk broke the peace.

Twisting in its direction on instinct, I stepped forward in anticipation of an attack, my hand already in my pockets for the holy book and my rosary.

Merry waved at me from behind the windshield of an old green Yukon, her smile broad before she stopped waving, petrified in the driver's seat.

"Where are we going?" The not-angel stood directly behind me, close enough her breath touched the side of my neck. She had opened her wings completely, sunshine catching in them.

A sigh escaped me at the notion of having to explain this in a few moments. "I don't know. Merry always has somewhere safe we can go. Let's just get in the wagon, right?" I ached for a joint, a drink—anything. We tossed our empty cups in the bin on the way.

I held up a hand to Merry the second I opened the passenger door in the back to allow Deevi time and space to fit her wings into the cab. Secured in the middle of the bench, I shut the door once she folded them, taking up the entire rear of the vehicle and crowding the groceries stuffed in the bay.

Merry didn't let me hold her back a second time when I climbed into the front. "That's an angel, Tater."

"No, I'm not," Deevi responded, annoyed. "And who's Tater?"

"I am." I made sure I put my seat belt on first. "Just fucking drive, Merry."

We got about half an hour toward Fort Lee on a Sunday morning when we hit traffic. A few drivers turned their attention our way, gaping at the mass of feathers covering the back windows of the Yukon before they continued wherever they were going.

Merry pushed in the cigarette lighter on the console. "Look in that glove box," she ordered me, remarkably calm.

I opened the compartment to find a sandwich bag stuffed to the seams with pre-rolls. "Merry!"

"Hand me one of them," she said. "We've gone too goddamn long with too little goddamn words said."

"Words for what?" Deevi piped in, sounding as innocent as the fresh day before us.

"We want to talk about you, but you're here," Merry and I said in unison, driven by the unknown power that had plagued me since I rescued the not-angel.

The priestess looked at me square, her eyes wide. "Tater!"

The lighter popped out with a click. I ripped open the bag and extracted one of the joints. "Just smoke until your eyes bleed. I'll do the talking."

Merry pulled out the glowing stick from the console, the joint bobbing from her lips while she tried to light its twisted end.

"Wait, wait, wait." I finally pulled out my burner. Unlocking the screen, my thumb slid open the voicemail alert.

Holding the phone to my ear, the Chair's Argentinian accent almost put me at ease.

"Patrick...Please call me. I am looking at pictures right now that defy

every ounce of my faith. You're in them. Please call me back. I'm sorry. It's clear that you were right, and God has put you on a path to Providence. Please call."

I whipped the phone away from my ear and tapped the camera app. Reversing the lenses, I held the phone up, making sure to get my tired ass in the shot with the heavenly being cramped in the backseat. She somehow had the wherewithal to smile at me at the perfect time, knowing full well I saw her too. I threw up the bird for extra spice.

I typed a text along with the photo.

CALL OFF THE GUARD. NOW.

Tapping send, I pressed down on the button to the electric window and almost threw the burner out of the car before the photo of Deevi and I caught me. Thinking for a moment, I deleted everything and tossed the phone on the street.

"What did you do that for?" the Vodun priestess asked, lips pinched to the pot.

"Insurance." I pushed the cigarette lighter back into its port before yanking the joint from Merry's mouth. A few quick draws filled my lungs with smoke. Deevi coughed in the backseat when I passed to the left.

Tugging on the bar on the right side of my seat, I looked back at the not-angel. "You have room?"

"Yes," she said, still smiling.

I tried to put on my best to match. Leaning the seat back, I took the next hit when Merry handed it over and closed my eyes after I handed it back to her. The radio came on. Christopher Wallace's divine speech and the thumping bass lines coaxed me to sleep in clouds of relief and a dreamless dark.

JERSEY

The smell of rubber, dust, and dank woke me when the Yukon's tire bumped a rock. I bolted upright to the sounds of endless, happy laughter.

Merry bent over the steering well, a burning stick hanging from her full lips while she rattled on. "The demon looked right at him and said 'What?'!"

Deevi's laughter rose, her arms hooked on Merry's seat while she threw her head back in joy.

After rubbing my face, I reached down and cranked the passenger seat up. "What are you two going on about?"

"Just telling old stories," Merry said, the smile on her face honest and wide. "We're almost there, by the way."

Outside the hot-boxed Yukon, the New Jersey countryside drank the last rays of the day as the sun, red and dull, dipped behind purple clouds and rolling hills. Corn fields swayed in the breeze, picturesque and beautiful for the uninitiated who didn't know any better. I hated the countryside; it's only in the country where one found the world's true evils. At least, it was in Italy. Merry drove us toward a farmhouse on some backroads east of Sussex.

I coughed in the haze she created. "How long have you been burning?"

"Since you fell asleep," said Deevi, her voice high and cheery. "Merry has been telling stories about the old days."

I glared at Merry, who chuckled at me like the lwas. "Oh, did you?"

"Not much of a choice, Tater," she said, holding the joint between her lips. She turned the big gray wheel in front of her to the right, swinging us off one dirt road for another. "Not every day I carry on conversations with angels."

"Ha, Tater." Deevi snorted. She tossed me a wink. "Later, Tater."

I fought a groan and faced forward.

The old farmhouse, gray and flaking, towered two levels with a tin roof that didn't match the palatial walls and wide bay windows. No curtains covered them, and the rooms within lay empty. No cars parked in the pebble lot before the old red barn that looked more appropriate to these bucolic climbs.

"Where the fuck are we, Merry?" I asked when we pulled to the front of the house.

"Old temple we sometimes use during festivals," she said, getting out the door. "We raise chickens here, too."

"Oh, chickens!" Deevi opened the bay door and burst out, planted on her feet like the Tasmanian Devil, excited beyond reason. She held her wings out in crazed, red-eyed anticipation. "Can I see the chickens?"

"They're in the barn now, girl. One of the laities came and closed up, so they are probably asleep." Merry searched her key ring, puttering forward. "Bring the bags, Tater."

"Tater," Deevi shouted, falling into laughter again.

"Aye, you're no angel," I muttered. Going around the back, I re-lifted the hatch to find three duffel bags stuffed to the seams. Rubbing the last of the sleep from my eyes, my shoulders nearly screamed when I hauled out the first two.

Deevi was standing right behind me when I turned. "Am I not your angel anymore?"

"Of course you are," I said, unable to consider anything else but the truth.

"But you said 'you're no angel', but you told me that I'm your angel. Which is it?"

On the verge of tears, she grabbed my shoulders, staking me to the spot. The weight of the bags tore at my hands and fingers, but the panic in her reddened eyes revealed all I needed to know. Thankfully, the question was too murky.

"What's wrong?" I asked, keeping my tone calm and even with the most powerful high person I'd ever encountered.

Deevi struggled to find words. She heaved a few times.

I dropped the bags in the dirt so I could lay my hands on her shoulders, linking us together. "Shhh. It's okay. It's okay."

Her grip tightened but she didn't hurt me. "I just want you to like me, Patrick. I don't want you to be mad at me."

"I'm not mad at you."

Night came, the stars speckling the sky.

She sniffed once and wiped her eyes with a finger and nodded. "Okay."

"Okay," I said. "Let's get you inside."

Deevi refused to let go of my hand as I led her through the empty kitchen and living rooms, wherein Merry caught me trying to sneak her through on the way to the staircase. Her ire died when she saw the leftover tears, and huffing, she marched outside to get the duffels.

Upstairs there were two bedrooms, both fully furnished, to my surprise, and better than most hotels. I switched on a bedside lamp and caught sight of a little Ogun statue in the corner, his mean old face glaring at me. Boxes of candles, bags full of herbs and dirt, drums —implements of ritual and devotion lay scattered around the room, a comfortable chamber any priest or priestess would love to call their own after nights of slaying hens. It was certainly better than my cell back in Rome when I had made time to be there, which was not often.

"Get some rest," I told Deevi.

She sat down on the bed, wiped her cheeks, and nodded. In the light of her wings, the room had brightened considerably, the glow of each feather complimenting every glisten, every scattering of warmth across the holy objects.

A shadow loomed in the corner of my vision. Stepping back, I whipped out my rosary.

Deevi looked in the corner where I stared. "Patrick?"

There was nothing there but old Ogun again, watching me as he watched all those that went to war with evil. Breathing all my frustrations through my nose, I forced a grin. "Just spooked for a moment, love. You get some rest, okay?"

She nodded, her frown deepening.

"What?" I asked. "At least this place isn't that basement, eh?"

"Am I still your angel?"

The urge to answer truthfully did not bite as hard this time. "Always."

Sniffling, she nodded and turned onto the bed, her wings folding around her like a cocoon of brightness. I backed out of the bedroom without another word, not wanting to aggravate or cause further conversation on the topic—knowing full well it waited for me downstairs in the kitchen.

Merry had unpacked one of the duffel bags she had dragged onto the kitchen table. Two bottles, one of whiskey and the other rum, held guard over fruits, vegetables, and those awful gluten-free snacks arrayed across the counter like a New York hipster's smorgasbord. Enough for three days before we had to go into a town, I grabbed the whiskey and twisted off the governor.

"Don't drink all of it," she said, standing at the kitchen sink. She stared out the window into the fresh night, lost in thought.

I plopped down at the table. "Felt it too, didn't you?"

"I couldn't help it." She fished out another hidden joint from the sewn pockets of her flower-print dress and sat down at the table with me. "It was like if I said something else, the outcome would be unbearable." Merry fumbled with the lighter before I took it and sparked us up.

"She's not an angel," I said while blowing out my first hit of smoke.

"She can't be. Neither heaven nor hell can walk the earth in physical forms."

"Neither can any lwas. It is why they possess," she whispered, wide-eyed before she exhaled a gout of smoke. "You and I have seen things most in this world don't want explained, Tater, let alone see in the first place. Rules are only rules until they are broken."

"Then it's clearly broken." I took the joint when she offered it. Drawing a puff, I blew out quick after letting the heat touch my throat. "You and I, or someone in one of our communities, would've said something if it ever had happened. And if angels can do it, why don't demons? Or the lwas? Or any of the real scary shit from the past?"

She bobbed her head in agreement after some thought, then paused. Her eyes locked with mine. "I only know one story of angels and the flesh."

And there it was: the worst fears of those who ruled the ancient world and the failed hopes of those who slaved under them. In Ireland, we envisioned Fomorians, one-legged and one-eyed, cursing us with plagues and death. The Norse thought them giants the gods put down, save those that escaped back to their homelands. I could have gone on about what the Hindus thought of the Adityas, or how Africans and Indigenous peoples the world over said this, that, or the other.

Instead, I thought of Enoch, and God sending him to slay the things I wished in that moment not to name. "Deevi's a Nephilim."

"She can't be." Merry shook her head, the white beads in her braids rattling around her shoulders. "Jehovah made those he spared spirits, and a few of them became his demons. But she can't be. Enoch wiped them out."

"Did he?" I asked. "She told me she grew up in Syria. What if..."

As always, she didn't let me drift into my own thoughts, thank God. "Get it out, Tater."

I swallowed my first slug of whiskey from the bottle, happy to let the burn give me time to think. The weed in my brain stem pushed past the endless ache of my body, the years racking bone and tendon alike. A thousand exorcisms flashed before my mind's eye, and I replayed every single one. If the demons could manifest, they wouldn't have ever needed those souls in the first place. They would have come and just taken what they wanted.

"What if she's been around since Enoch?" I finally worked out.

Merry laughed at the question. "She's so young. Naive, even. All she wanted to do during the ride here was ask questions about you. After a while, I didn't stop, and she just sat there and listened to every word. She asked things about you that I shouldn't have told her, and things that you would be too embarrassed to let anyone know about save me."

"Ah, fuck, I knew you two were up to something more when I woke up."

The coal at the end of the joint flared red as she sucked another hit, her eyes already pinked. "I think she's in love with you."

"Shut up." Plucking the stick from her lips, I took a big lungful of smoke and exhaled, leaning over to look at the wooden floor of the kitchen beneath my feet. "Just—just shut up."

"So she got to you."

The sadness in her voice made me squint hard, hoping beyond hope that when I opened them, I'd be somewhere else. "She did not. There's just something weird about her."

"Your heart's actually beating?" she asked, amused.

"Merry!"

"Tater!" She slapped her thighs. "You don't act like this around other women. You don't act like this around me!"

"Act like what?"

"Like you're possessed."

Merry and I ceased to speak for the rest of the evening.

11

———

MORNING STARS

The warmth woke me first, a breath of light and movement that saved my night from the most horrible dreams.

Demons clawed past the faces of so many souls, so many patients, if I remembered them right. The more illusions they cast, the deeper I sank into the morass of damnation. The innocent twisted and changed, horns sprouting from their foreheads while their natural teeth popped out, replaced by bloody, gnashing fangs. Hands into claws, talons black and deep, tore flesh from my face as I tried to say the Lord's Prayer.

Our Father, who art in heaven... hallowed be thy name. Thy kingdom come, thy will be done, on earth as it is in heaven. Give me not to temptation, but deliver me from evil, for thine is the kingdom, the power, and the...

I tried five times before I stopped and completed the Rosary in Irish, the first rays of morning forcing my eyes open.

I had passed out on the patchwork couch in the living room. In my briefs and barefoot, the chill on my flesh made me look for the blanket Merry had given me before she had marched upstairs last night. It lay on the floor only a few feet away. I leaned out to grab a corner when I felt the breeze wash over me again.

The front door to the house lay open.

Cursing under my breath, I let go of the wool and reached for my pants, sliding on my dirty jeans and sticking both feet into my damp boots. Closing the door as I went outside, I cursed a second time and turned back for the threadbare couch, searching for my rosary and my Bible that had fallen in the cracks between the red-green cushions. The cold chill of the morning had snuck into the living room by then, prickling my skin to the point where I threw on my coat, too.

The sun waited on the gray horizon and the fresh dew hung in crystal clouds that weighed upon this valley deep in the heart of New Jersey. Dairy cows grazed in cornfields cut down for the season so their shit could replenish the soil. Frost on the grass gleamed in the gold-orange light. The trees shifted in the frozen wind.

I searched the sky and pawed my jeans' pocket, feeling the hard outline of a lighter and something softer. Fishing them out, I recovered the little blue Bic and small blunt I had rolled while Merry and I drank in the kitchen. The vegetative stink of the sativa hit my head in a rush, bringing me to while the smoke warmed my chest and throat. My search of the skies yielded nothing.

Until I spotted her.

Deevi flew over a grove of oak, ash, and thorn on the other side of the field, circling with a hawk in the sky.

Mesmerized for a moment by the uncanny sight, I made toward her. My boots crunched broken stalks that smelled of rot. More puffs, more warmth. There was a unique sensation to that day so far from where I had started all this.

The not-angel on high, clad only in her panties and the wife-beater I had bought with stolen credit cards, promised no good ends.

But this damned urge kept me moving forward.

Why her?

Heaven help me, I didn't know. I didn't look at her like I looked at any of the women I had ever been with, even my first wife in my first life back in Ireland when shit rained from the sky itself and she was my Zipporah. Deevi was glory and perfection and beauty and wonder and fantasy, yet she also carried damnation and lusts and doubts and impossibilities and a smile that would make me forsake my faith in God if she asked.

In an instant.

Was that love or sin? Was I already damned?

My tears of terror dried with the end of my blunt. Tucking the lighter into my pocket, I entered the wood. Picking past thickets and broken bushes, the rotted stench grew heavier the closer I came to the center.

A fox picked at the carcass of a deer well into its decay. He lifted his head when he heard me stomp into the glade, his fuzzy face dyed red. Our eyes met, his golden rings bewitching me. Licking black lips, his white teeth gnashed bloody bits before he smacked his mouth. He suddenly stilled, studying me more deeply than I did him.

Something about that little bastard's gaze dug deeper, seeking out something until, by a piece of what I hope was imagination, he smiled at me.

"Careful, careful," the fox whispered. "I'm watching you, Patrick."

"Patrick?"

I literally jumped out of one of my boots, bringing my fists up as if it would have mattered.

Deevi stood beside me, watching with amused, loving curiosity. "Are you alright?"

Back over my shoulder, the fox had escaped. For some reason, laughter, far away and fading, echoed in the back of my head. I faced her. "I'm okay."

"You and Merry smoked a lot last night."

I chuckled, rubbing the top of my head with a cold hand.

The silence between us pervaded like the stink of the rotted deer. I avoided her eyes before because of that damned urge, but this time I suddenly met her golden stare.

She smiled at me.

I went right into it. "You said you grew up in Syria, yeah?"

That smile withdrew a bit. "Do you think I will lie to you?"

I didn't even hesitate against it. "I don't think you've been entirely clear and that's been on purpose, love. We can't get on like that."

Deevi nodded, her tanned hands folded in front of her waist.

"What is your mother's name?"

The question made her pause. "Lisbeth."

"And your father is an angel." Nut-cutting time. "You're a Nephilim."

"Yes." She reached up and tugged on a lock of her dark hair. "My father is among the angels and my mother was human. I grew up in a monastery in Syria."

"Who raised you? Your father?"

"No, a church. The Holy Roman Catholic Church," she said without a second thought. "At least that is what the nuns told me."

Those bastards.

Those fucking bastards. They sent a fucking fire team after me to reclaim property. They did this. They must have been why I was there.

I wonder if the Chair had bullshitted me the entire time. A shake of my hands to force warmth back into them refocused me. "How did you end up in America?"

"One day, one of the nuns came to me and said that Father Lucius wanted to meet me, and that he was a very important man. He said that I needed to come with him," she recalled, seeking out the memories in the gory carrion beyond me. Deevi's wings remained completely still. "I got on a boat, and he had his bishops take me to the place where you found me. They left me there."

"Father Lucius," I echoed, committing the name to memory. "What did they say to you? Anything?"

"No," she said. "They just left me there."

The loneliness in her voice broke my heart. "Sorry. They shouldn't have done that."

"You found me," she said, crossing her arms as if she might shiver, but she never did. "And I'm fine now. I'm safe."

Nodding in agreement, I stuck both hands into the pockets of my black peacoat, rocking my feet in my boots to create some friction against the chill seeping in my toes. "Are you the only one? You know, of your kin?"

"I never met any others."

"Okay, time for double jeopardy." I squared my stance with hers, letting the weed's numbness steady me for a brief second. "How old are you?"

"Patrick!"

"Deevi, I gotta know."

"But I don't."

The noise she made, a slight whimper of frustration, stopped me in my tracks. I heard her sniff to keep herself together, like a soldier who had just been given the worst order. She didn't know: she had never left Syria, wherever they had her. She had never worn clothes like the rest of us, or had her first drink, or made love, or gone to school, listened to the radio, did sneaky stuff with boys or girls after class…

She had been left alone. Perhaps for a long time.

"How many nuns do you know?" I asked, trying something simple.

"I've forgotten some of their names. They were my friends, and I can't remember."

With a duck past her wing, I took her hand, guiding Deevi about to face me dead-on. "I don't know what happened either, but that doesn't matter right now. What does is that you're here, you're okay, and you're going to be okay."

"Yes," she said with a nod. "I'm going to be okay."

"Aye. Aye, you are."

We held hands and watched the new day come through the trees, the white rays caught in the fog. For a moment, it looked like a chilly day in County Wicklow. The thought of home warmed me.

Deevi dropped my hand and glanced behind us. Studying the thicket I had hiked through, her shoulders twitched in that direction. "Merry is calling."

"What? What's wrong?"

"She's calling you. She's shouting your name."

I ran as hard as I could, my angel flying above to get out ahead of me on our way back to the farmhouse. My lungs ached with my legs by the time we reached the front porch to find the priestess standing there with her smartphone, the screen brightening her beautiful face as she watched in terror. The commentator of the news clip rambled on.

"What?" I asked her, bent over with my hands on my knees to catch my breath in the cold.

Merry glanced up from her phone when Deevi landed beside me. She stared hard at her before she spoke. "C-come look."

Ascending the first step, I took the phone from her shaking hands. Merry sat down as I flipped the screen in my direction, the picture spinning clockwise to orient itself.

St. Peter's Basilica billowed black smoke, the robin's egg dome shattered down to its wider, sturdier base. Hundreds of people ran from the church, tourists mixed in with black and red robed priests, who, for the good in them, held their place among the fleeing crowds to direct them toward quicker avenues of escape.

I almost dropped the phone. The ticker beneath the images ran quickly, repeating the same story again and again.

POPE ATTACKED IN ST. PETER'S. SATANISTS CLAIM VICTORY FROM THE COUNTRYSIDE. 27 DEAD. POPE'S WHEREABOUTS UNKNOWN AT THIS TIME.

"Oh, no," I said, whispering it under my breath. Thankfully I turned in time so my ass slammed on the porch's bottom step, my legs going out from under me. "Oh, no."

Someone had attacked the Chair.

I let my hands hang between my legs as Merry and Deevi clucked over me like hens, prodding me for information, explanations, words. The phone's weight slid in my palms, my entire body numbed.

The Nephilim's voice cut through. "Say something, Patrick."

"Why you?" I asked Deevi, devoid of any feeling. "God had his champion wipe out all the Nephilim. Why were you spared?"

"Tater!" Merry bolted me in the arm with a hard jab. "You can't ask that."

"I need to ask that." I stood up, causing both of them to back away. Freezing in my boots, my upper body goose-fleshed when another breeze tore through, carrying the smell of wood smoke. I stepped closer to Deevi, a horrid question on the tip of my tongue. "Who's your Da?"

Deevi hesitated, her wings drooping like a dog's tail. For the sorrow in my heart at seeing her fret, I pushed it away.

"Tell me," I said again. "Who's your da?"

She braved at the word, standing a bit taller. "His name is Lucifer. My father's name is Lucifer Morningstar."

Merry and I stood there, unblinking before the phone in my hand buzzed. Looking down at the screen, an unexpected name popped up.

SAINT GEORGE.

12

FAMILY GUY

The battered black Escalade bounced down the dirt path to the barn, the sun settling behind the hills it had roared atop before rolling down the other side. The Englishman and I saw each other, even at a distance. A prickle of anticipation worked up the center of my back.

"Do we tell him?" Merry asked, seated beside me on the steps.

We cradled paper cups full of bourbon in our hands, the only warmth there would be against a cloudy night. The heater had blown, and I was too drunk to go collect wood for the fireplace. "He's going to know the moment he sees the wings," I said, summoning the will for a long sip. The taste of charred wood burnt my tongue in a flaming tang, joining the potatoes and jerk chicken Merry had cooked for lunch.

"Not her wings, dummy," she said, taking another puff from what had to be our fifth blunt for the day.

Thank God we had them. "Oh, that."

"That is different," she continued. "One thing to deal with a Nephilim, but Lucifer's daughter?"

"I guess Beherit had a good reason for sending me on this goose-chase."

"You really see it that way?"

I gave no answer as George's truck pulled up a few yards from the porch. Getting out, he stood there like the posh ponce he was, trying his best to rankle a bruised and battered face to the beauties around us. For some reason beyond me, the stupid idiot clutched his sword by the throat in its scabbard, on full display. He pinched a black folder under his arm on the opposite side.

"Very rustic," he said. He left the car door open, the first sign he had another weapon in the front. Probably an assault rifle, knowing the crazy git. "Are you truly here alone, Patrick?"

"Just me, my voodoo mama, and our Nephilim," I replied, waving away the joint when Merry amusingly tried to offer it to me. She knew when to play along.

George stared daggers at her. "Is she to remain?"

"This is my house, white boy," Merry quickly answered. "And you'd best remember I'm not the only one watching here. You walk upon the spirits of my people."

"Charming." George stepped away from his vehicle and shut the driver's side door, carrying no more than what he had brought. "Where is she?"

I shook my head. "Updates first."

"You said she was here." The anger left his bruised face, replaced by a clear, open curiosity.

I remembered where we both grew up reading the same books, being told the same things. He needed a bit of faith.

Reaching out for the joint, I nodded to the Dragonslayer after Merry gave it over. "I guess we can have a look."

The stinking cloud I made him walk through on our way to the cornfields gave him a little cough. "I see you're still with your sins."

"Is God's creation truly a sin?"

"Some things take us from the Lord and into the Devil's arms."

I cracked a knowing grin that caused George to bristle. "And some of us actually keep that Fifth Commandment."

"Some of us will be forgiven for the depth of our devotion."

That was all I needed. Grabbing him by the lapels of his fancy gray jacket, I turned him onto the cream vinyl siding of the house. His arms drawn up to guard his head, I laughed loudly as I kneed George right in the balls. He tried to bellow something, but the wind leaving him reduced it to a wheeze. On his side, a kick to the chest for good measure sealed off any chance for him to make a comeback.

I jerked him up and pressed him against the house again, dragging him to the corner.

"Look! Look there," I said, pointing off in the distance.

Huffing to find his breath, George turned his wrathful, pained glare away from me. He had the heat zapped from him in an instant.

Deevi flew over the rotted grove at the end of the dead fields, her wings shining like shards of glass in the sunset. Thankfully, I had talked her into a pair of sweatpants, but no amount of cloth could diminish her glory.

"She's not to be fucked with," I said, my nose pressed into George's shaved cheek. "Do you get me?"

Wordless, George nodded. I shoved myself off of him and marched for the heath.

He caught up to me a few yards later, stumbling. "She's...she's real!"

"Aye, she is. But you don't forget—my angel is no angel. She's a Nephilim, heaven and earth joined, the first of this world's heroes and its monsters. If she asks you a question, you will answer."

"Who shall force me?"

"You shall, brother George."

He kept his mouth shut for the rest of the walk.

Deevi landed on the broken earth when we reached the grove's border where the dead corn gave way to crabgrass under the outlying trees. For all his bravado, George stayed silent, awed by her mere presence until she spoke.

"Is this the man you told me about?" she asked me.

I nodded.

She hummed at the Englishman's appearance. She stepped forward, only a foot or two separating them, and offered her hand. "I'm Deevi."

"G-George," he said, accepting it.

"Nice to meet you, George," Deevi responded with a clean smile. "Were you the one that tried to stop Patrick from saving me?"

He tried to pull his hand out of hers, a distinct visage of terror on his face when he blurted out, "I was."

Deevi jerked George back in front of her. "You will never do that again. Do you understand why?"

"Because you'll kill me."

"Exactly," she said, dropping his hand.

I worked hard to suppress the cackle rising in my chest. She was damn Wonder Woman. "Okay, okay, let's be at peace. You've seen her now, Georgie. What's this information you said you had over the phone?"

Flexing his right hand open and shut, he pulled the file out from under his armpit. "This was in my hotel the day after your incident with the Swiss Guard. I think the Chair got it to me before it all went up."

I took the black folder and opened it and immediately bent down to catch a small shape that fell out of the spine. My hand closed around a thumb-drive, its black plastic carved in the relief of Mary with the Body. For some reason, the damned thing bothered the skin of my palm, as if ants bit me.

"What's this?" I tossed the thumb-drive at George.

He caught it out of the air against his chest. "All of the Vatican's Archives, down to the catacomb vaults. The paper is just what they've found so far."

"Did you not read it yet?" I asked, annoyed.

"Pardon for being too busy worrying about the faith of the Church!" George scoffed and snatched the file back out of my hands, deciding to keep all the materials together for the sake of his dickishness. "It says that this New Word cult you discovered while tramping around New York is the name for a rumored movement the Vatican has been following on the Dark Web."

Still annoyed, I tucked my irritated hand into my pocket. "Get to the point."

"Our information is spotty, to say the least, but our best interpretation..." George glanced at Deevi before averting his eyes to the ground.

"Get it out," I said.

"It's so damnable I dare not utter it, Patrick," he said.

"What does this New Word want with me?" Deevi asked.

"They'd use you to breed the Antichrist." Shuddering at his inability to control himself, George scrunched his face in confusion. "Please don't ask me for more."

"Why?" she pressed before I said anything.

George fought to keep his mouth closed, pursing his lips before the truth broke free. "They wish to bring on the End of Days and the coming of God's kingdom."

"But why?" I asked. "All those Satanists talk about wanting to bring the Devil into the world, but none of them actually want to when it comes to killing time. They all know how it ends for them."

"They're not Satanists," said George.

"Then what are they?" I checked on Deevi.

She stood there, not a hair or feather out of place, but her eyes had changed. Just like with demons, her pupils had grown larger in each passing instant, until only a sliver of the whites remained. I wondered then if real angels would look like that if they possessed someone. Instead of wrath and vengeance against their maker, I imagine they'd look upon us with disappointment.

And that was what lay in her eyes. It broke my heart.

"They're Christians, Patrick," George said. "Damned evangelical Christians."

13

RUBBERS

Christians overthrew the Chair, cut off the March of Saints, and now worked toward the End of Days.

The reality of it, easier to accept at face value than I liked, did nothing to comfort Deevi while we sat at the kitchen table well past midnight. George had passed out on the couch in the living room, taking my bed without asking. Merry had retreated upstairs with the bottle of rum and half the blunts she had. I had a feeling I wouldn't see her for a day or two.

Deevi stared at the vinyl between us, a fold of worry at the corner of her mouth.

Tired of the silence, the pause, I went to the kitchen counter and the bottle of whiskey. Taking two paper Dixie cups as well, I brought it back to the table and sat down again, this time at the end beside her. Open went the bottle, drizzle went the whiskey.

I slid a cup over to Deevi.

"What's this?" she asked.

I signaled for her to take it. "A drink. Sometimes we need a drink."

After a moment of hesitation, she brought the shot up to her lips and sipped. She made a foul face. "This is awful."

"You'll get a taste for it." I downed my shot in a single gulp and refilled, pouring more into the little paper cup. The Green Spot warmed its way down into my chest.

Deevi attempted her second sip and did not wince as much this time, letting the whiskey roll around her mouth before she swallowed. "Why do your people make this?" she asked, making another sour face.

"Man loves the wonder of God's creation and the things we can do with it. The alchemy of the fruit is sometimes as wonderful as the fruit itself."

"Is it?"

"What?"

Deevi took a third sip. "If man was made to shepherd God's wonders, did God give them permission to slaughter the flocks? Or breed the cows and horses, making and remaking them until they aren't what they were? Did he give them permission to perform 'alchemy'?"

"Deevi," I said, gentle against the multiple compulsions tugging me with each question. "Not all of them are like that."

"But some are." Her mouth opened and closed, struggling to find words before the truth, a horrible, heartbreaking truth fell out. "Some of them want to rape me."

What did one say to the divine when their divine heart was broken? Being taught to consider the Great Mystery with every rosary often left more members of the clergy questioning rather than considering. I wondered why—how—the Lord led me to her, or allowed her, or allowed any of this shit. "God works in mysterious ways."

As if that made it any fucking better when I said it out loud.

I don't know if God was with me anymore at that point, or if He had ever truly been with any saints in the first place. We suffered, we bled, and we died for Him. He didn't make us holy; others did, with him only signing off.

Do nods nobody sees equal action?

No disrespect to the Son, but the Father failed me again.

For that reason alone, I don't know why I had one of my better moments. Reaching across the table, I laid my hand on hers, lacking for a better answer.

Her tanned hand clapped atop of mine, warm and sure. I broke her grip and went for it, turning my hand up so we could come together, fingers laced tightly until the spaces between ached. The urge to pull her across the table, or to try, and give into these damned feelings, sins, screamed at me to submit.

She came at me first, mounting my lap after turning around the chair I sat in. Lips tasting of cinnamon mashed against mine. Bliss captured me, inescapable and intense, beyond any words, thought, or deed.

My hands laid on the soft fabric of the sweatpants over her hips while Deevi wrapped her arms around my head, kissing my cheeks, lips. I traced my fingers beneath the edge of her white wife-beater, finding the smooth skin of her lower back.

I tore my lips from hers. "I can't."

"Why not?" Deevi whispered, nibbling on my ear.

That damned urge.

Because I wouldn't stop. Because I couldn't.

"Because I'm not worth it."

Deevi leaned back in my arms and held my face, catching me dead in the eyes. "Why?"

For once, the urge couldn't force easy truths. The words came anyway.

"Because I'm not a good man. I'm a fool and a drunk and a pothead and a fornicator and I take God's name in vain, and I don't feel like I've ever really saved anyone, let alone myself. I don't know if God loves me or not, and I'm just trying to do his will. I'm trying and I'm failing. And here you come, and for some reason…" For the first time I was happy that tears actually stopped my breath. "I love you. I don't know why, but I have since the moment you said your name. I don't know why but I can't help it, because honest to Christ, I don't want to fuck you. It feels wrong, and rash, and we don't have no rubbers."

She broke out in laughter. Loud, happy laughter.

Holding my face, she wiped my tears away with her thumbs, and once again the inescapable claimed me. Holiness personified, it was more than just her beauty or words—she was a creature of grace, who if left alone would save the lost, right wrongs, and heal men's souls.

Her laughter healed my broken heart.

"What are rubbers?" she asked, pressing her forehead to mine.

"Condoms." Her confusion made me chuckle a bit. "Vests for your Jimmy. Sleeves. Wraps. Seventy-five Cent Insurance."

"Where do you learn all these words?"

"Urban Dictionary and Dr. Dre."

She shook her beautiful head, dark tresses fluttering. "I don't know what those are."

Suddenly all the lights in the house popped on. Phones buzzed on tables as their screens woke, televisions upstairs blared, and the radio by the sink crackled. The bulb in the fixture above the kitchen table beside us exploded, raining shards of glass that Deevi deflected with a quick fan of her wings.

More shattering. Merry screamed my name from upstairs while George cussed a storm, the both of them stomping around in a panic.

A voice came on all the sets and speakers in the house. It was calm, collected, and quite assured.

"My name is Thomas Cromwell. I'll thank you to pay attention to what I'm about to say, because I'll only say it once: give me the Nephilim. Now."

14

NAMES

The smiling face on my smart phone's screen gazed out in confidence, tanned and shaved smooth save for a pair of perfect brows and a haircut that cost more than a fancy dinner. Thomas Cromwell stared at the camera from wherever he was sitting for a long time, his pale blue eyes fixed as if he saw the viewers beyond it.

As if he saw me.

"Bring her back to New York," he said in his smooth Kentucky accent. "Just leave her in a park. Or at a subway stop. Or just stay where you are. Either way, we're coming."

The screens of the phones on the kitchen table winked off with the power in the house, leaving Deevi and I in the dark kitchen, littered in broken glass. Stepping back from me, her bare feet crunched on the shards.

I winced at the sound. "Don't!"

She held out a hand to calm me. "It's okay." She crunched some more, stomping to show me her imperviousness.

"Can you get my boots?" I asked, just accepting it.

At that moment, Merry and George barged into the kitchen, the latter leading the way with his sword unsheathed.

"We're fine," I called when they entered. Deevi marched around the kitchen table and found my Docs by the door, bringing them over as Merry blustered.

"Look at my fucking kitchen," the Vodun priestess cried, on the border of the shard field. "That motherfucker! That motherfucker! I'm going to kill him!"

"Just…" I turned over my boots and shook them out. "Do you have a broom?"

Merry gave me a hard look, the kind one doesn't want a Haitian woman giving them. She turned and stalked through the house.

George rested his sword on the floor, point down, and knelt with it. "There's nobody else here, Patrick."

"What do you mean?" Deevi asked, standing guard behind me with her hands on my shoulders.

George didn't miss it. "These manifestations are not uncommon events to behold in an exorcism."

"But there's no demon here," I finished, drawn to a horrific conclusion. I finally blinked a few times before I turned my boots over and knocked my fists on the treads, doing my damnedest to empty them as much as possible. "Go get your cart started, Georgie."

"Where are we going?" Merry asked when she walked right back into the kitchen, wearing a garish pair of tie-dye platform boots that looked like something Huggy Bear Brown left behind as she dragged a shop-vac behind her.

"You're staying here with Deevi," I answered. "We need to keep her out of the city at all costs. Farther if need be."

Merry dropped the vacuum hose. "You can't just leave me here!"

"Stop shouting," I shouted back at her.

"Patrick, where are you going?" asked Deevi, somehow calmer than us mortals.

Merry almost cackled as the words came flooding out of me. "George and I are going to New York. Whoever this bastard is, he's possessed by something powerful enough that they reached out and found us."

"And staying here means he knows where we are," George said. "We have to leave this place as soon as we possibly can."

"Aye, boyo," I said. "I want Merry to stay here with Deevi and get this place packed. You and I will go back to the city and figure this out."

"How?" Merry asked. "If this Cromwell is so powerful, what is splitting up going to do, Fred?"

"We're not splitting up, Velma." I nodded at George to go get his SUV going and, to my surprise, he did so without a word of protest. I turned and watched him go, only to find Deevi waiting for me beside the door. "You two wait for me to call in a few hours. I'll let you know where we'll meet up," I said. "We'll put it all to Mary."

Our bug-out phrase. Merry paused for the barest moment then nodded, the fight gone from her. "See you there."

Deevi stood there by the exit, the light of her wings setting the shards on the floor agleam. She took my hand in hers as we passed, jerking me to a halt when I tried to leave without saying anything.

"Will you be careful?"

I didn't fight against the truth. "Never been good at it."

Her expression remained without emotion, and her grip on my hand slackened.

I held firm. "You still have that burning sword?"

Deevi perked at the question. "Like my faith."

"Then keep it with you. I'll be back soon."

We struggled not to do it, to step forward and join our lips together. I still tasted her, and for all the yearning in my heart to get away, I wanted more.

She braved the distance and kissed me. Softly, gently, and with love.

I refused to meet anyone's gaze, behind or before me, as I pounded down the front steps of the farmhouse and into George's SUV.

"Did you just kiss her?" the Englishman growled at me while I buckled into the passenger seat.

"Just get the fuck on, all right?"

The Escalade rumbled down the dirt road beneath a sky black with clouds. Ahead lay endless darkness that our headlights didn't push away for the brief moment, the uneven earth beneath us and the A/C sucking the smell of dusk, the only clue that we had not fallen into a void.

George broke the silence first. "What are you doing here, Patrick? How did you get here?"

"I don't know." I didn't have anyone else to talk to that would understand, and no matter how much we played at hating each other, we were still brothers under God and all the things we had done.

So he took my confession.

I told him everything, from Beherit back in Italy after I ditched the Vatican to the bar in Brooklyn to finding Deevi all the way to us driving in the car. I still left out the fact that Lucifer was her father. He drove us onto the highway before I finished, and when I did, the silence returned.

"So why were you kissing her?" He asked when he had the floor.

"I don't know."

"Say the Lord's Prayer."

"Why the fuck do I need to do that?"

"You know why." George let his attention to the road waver to stare warnings at me.

I sighed and signed. "Our Father, who art in heaven, hallowed be thy name, thy kingdom come, thy will be done, on earth as it is in Heaven. Give us this day our daily bread and forgive our trespasses as we forgive those who trespass against us. Lead us not to temptation, but deliver us from evil, for thine is the kingdom, the power, and must I?"

He snorted. "Fine. So, what's the plan?"

"We'll get to the island and ditch this for something easier. I have an idea of where we're going."

"Pray tell."

"It's an idea," I said, reaching down for my seat's crank. I leaned it back and put my hands behind my head. The void continued, broken by the revelation of the highway, its painted yellow lines, and the constant hum. The vibration threatened sleep to my tired, heavy eyes, and I realized how long I had gone drinking and smoking without really eating or taking water.

And I couldn't finish the Lord's Prayer.

I couldn't finish it no matter how hard I tried.

PART II

THE SERPENT AND THE ROOSTER

15

UBER DOS

George ditched the Escalade somewhere in Hoboken before we took the train back into Midtown Manhattan. We stayed underground for the next few hours on the subway, riding the tunnels in search of donuts and coffee shops, feasts provided by his functioning black card. Fat and free for the time-being, we let rush hour go by before we hustled the lines again.

He and I bickered on the cross streets to Yeshiva University in Murray Hill.

"We should be going to the closest diocese," he argued with me. "They will have the things we need to storm Bar Rochelle."

"The last thing I'm fucking giving you is a gun in a fucking night-club." I mashed at the application icon on the screen of my burner with my thumb. Uber finally loaded. "And with the Chair gone we can't assume anything."

"Then why are we getting picked up at a synagogue?" George asked. He carried his sword in an old lacrosse bag, every bit the private school asshole he was, but we went to the same school, so I didn't bother to make the point.

"How much do you ever hear about Jewish exorcisms?" I asked.

Our ride pulled up twelve minutes later. To my surprise, I recognized the gunmetal gray Corolla. The passenger side window rolled down.

"Patrick?" Tina called out to me, clad in the exact same tight gray dress suit.

I bent down and looked right at her pretty face. "Hiya, Tina! Seems like this is a small world, aye?"

"I guess so," she said with a comfortable laugh. "Do you have a friend this time?"

"He's a colleague." I slid into the passenger seat and strapped in. "Say hi, Georgie."

George sulked into the backseat.

"So off to exorcise more demons today?" Tina asked as she pulled away from the curb.

There was a faint scent of burnt tobacco in the cabin this time— not that Tina made any note of it or paid attention beyond waiting for my response. We all hid our little stresses, and as the red brick and trash-strewn alleys passed by outside my window, I knew this city created more than its fair share. "Exactly that."

"Oh, you told her," George cawed from the backseat. "Of course, you did."

"What's his problem?" Tina asked, glancing in her rearview.

"Don't mind him. He's repressed."

She settled forward. "Oh-kay. So how goes the fight against the Devil?"

"Not even the Devil we're fighting," I said. "It's the Christians this time."

"Excuse me?" asked Tina.

"Remember when you dropped me off in Brooklyn, love?"

She responded to my question with an unsteady nod, her eyes on the road. "Sure."

"Well," I began, slapping my bent knees, "wouldn't you believe it, my voodoo priestess lover summoned the spirits of her people, and they led me to a club in Brooklyn just filled to the brim with the damned. Oh, you should have seen them—Gothed-out, clubbed-out, and completely full of themselves. Anyway, we got to talking, and they led me to a Nephilim."

George exploded in the backseat. "Saint Patrick of Ireland!"

I glanced back at him. "Shush, you."

"What's a Nephilim?"

"Don't you dare," George warned me. "Don't you dare."

"Imagine if an angel and a human had a baby. Her name's Deevi."

"You told me that angels and demons couldn't take physical form," Tina replied after a few moments.

"Oh, good, she was listening," shouted George, kicking the back of my seat.

I twisted around and pointed my finger right in his face. "Quiet down, you limey fuck, or I'll have her pull this car over. Don't kick her seats."

He seethed at me but said nothing.

An awkward silence followed us across the east side of the island and over the bridge again, past streets beginning to bustle with the hustle of America. Mexicans went to work on cranes while Irish tore up narrow roads, halting our traffic down to where I could spot the Nigerian and Indian cab drivers that seemed to helm every yellow taxi. Women in blazers and tight dress skirts marched the granite slab sidewalks, floating on the points of their three-inch designer heels that would wear out in a week, but they compared nowhere near to the pomp and pageantry of the men, many of them suited so resplendently that if they were demons I wouldn't have been able to tell.

Demons love clothes, for some odd reason.

Tina turned us down the avenue to Bar Rochelle in Brooklyn sometime later, her brown eyes searching the world ahead of us for answers it wouldn't give.

Strangely, I fretted over her silence. Before Deevi, before the lwas, there had been nothing I wanted more than to be left alone. Being able to confess the truth, to tell someone else what was happening, no matter if they thought I was crazy, helped me more on that car ride than sitting in a booth would have.

More so since she didn't believe me.

Tina spoke. "Are you fucking with me again, Patrick?"

"I told you the first time," I replied. "I'm true."

She looked at George in the rearview. "Is he?"

"Don't fucking talk to me," George said.

"Ooooo-kay." Tina glanced at me. "Are you both exorcists?"

"Yep," I said.

"So I guess you're going to go exorcise more demons," she guessed.

I nodded.

"And you recently freed a Nerf-el-what?"

"A Nephilim. A child of an angel and a human."

"They didn't teach us about those in Sunday School," Tina said.

"They don't actually teach you anything in Sunday School," I said, looking down the street. In the daylight, the sign for Bar Rochelle stood black and dull. The unlit fluorescents spelling out the club's name might have been the newest bits added since they put the damn thing up however long ago.

Tina pulled her Corolla beside two sedans parked by the busy curb. George slid out without even a word of thanks, leaving her and I to the silence of the cabin and the roar of New York's streets outside.

Unbuckling my seat belt, I reached for the door's handle. "See you, Tina."

"Patrick?"

She was looking dead at me when I stooped down. "Yes?"

"You told me you're true, right?"

"Right as rain."

"Then I think you should use Lyft from now on," Tina responded.

She sped away without another word or even a farewell, another person lost to mundane willingness.

"At least she sees you're a wanker," George said.

The mud brown doors to Bar Rochelle were shut, the handles chained together with a heavy padlock. I stuck my cold hands in the pockets of my coat and glanced up the street, spotting the sign for an upscale pizzeria which championed their free Wi-Fi.

"Just get on," I finally responded, heading that way. "We'll be back at dark when they open."

16

PIZZA PARTY

We sat in the pizzeria for hours while we played with George's smart phone to find all we could on Thomas Cromwell. That smile of his, sure and confident of its purpose, had seared itself in my mind. It surprised me when we found the chap's profile on Wikipedia, of all places.

"Born in Louisville, attended Wharton with the president before entering Liberty University, this man regularly serves his congregation of over seven million-strong at his New Word Fellowship," George rattled off as he scanned the screen, reading much like he had in our school days. "Good lord, this man has access to a president. And the wrong one too."

"That does not surprise me," I said, wiping my face with my jacket sleeve after devouring a third slice of pepperoni.

"...and the Pope."

"Makes sense. They would have known the Vatican's layout to topple the Chair the way they did. I bet they've been scoping them for a while."

George grunted in agreement.

"How much is the bastard worth?"

He dragged his thumb up the screen and paused. "You don't want to know."

I chuckled and leaned on the bar counter next to the display cases where they kept the pies, the exhaustion of the last…I don't know how much time had really passed since the moment I found Deevi in that basement, but the time weighed, nonetheless.

The lass behind the register came over, making her rounds. "Anything more, gentlemen?" she asked, her blonde dyed hair put up in an attractive bun. "We'll be opening our bar in a few minutes."

"What's your Irish?" I asked.

"I have some Green Spot," she said.

"Four shots, then," I said before flicking my head in George's direction. "He's got it."

She smiled at my current partner in holiness, which caught his eye as she walked away.

"We're not here to get drunk," he said after his gaze lingered.

"Oi, just a few drinks. And don't tell me you don't like that girl eyeing you."

If George's glare could kill, he'd have murdered me on the spot. His cheeks reddened. "It doesn't matter."

"Because of this, that, and the other piece of scripture, I'm guessing," I replied in mock boredom.

"Because that is the law of the Vatican established long ago, and we are not above God's decrees when they are handed down from high," he said, glowering. "And some of us take our vows seriously, Patrick, though I don't think you'd understand that."

I tried my best not to roll my eyes. There was nothing more tired than English condescension, especially out in the open. "Last time I checked, I'm still pulling demons out of people like you are, and God hasn't…"

He broke my pause. "Well, go on."

Unable to carry my thought into words, I shook my head. "No, never mind."

"No, Patrick," George said with an inquisitor's fervor. "What hasn't God done for you?"

Our waitress returned with my four shots of whiskey, but said nothing nor offered that smile again, noticing how the man beside me fumed. Part of me wanted to slide back off the stool I sat on and belt George across the face like I had a few nights ago, but the question remained and would remain until I found an answer for myself, not just him.

"I don't know. The Lord leads me—and you—to and fro and all over this blue ball, and for every person I free from Satan's hold, the less sure I am that what we're doing Gods works."

He groaned.

"Listen." I grabbed two of the shots the blonde with the bun had left and slid them over to George, who looked at them as if I had handed him something from another planet. The two I kept for me stayed right in front, and the first went down with a burn that sledgehammered its way to my gut. "We keep saving these people who give themselves to the Devil, and for all the bloody good it does, there's always more of them choosing to turn toward the dark. And look what we've been told about that dark! Last week, did you think there was a Nephilim just bobbing around the world, cuter than can be?"

George glanced at his portions of potion.

I could tell by the way he pressed his lips together I had dug deep. "God hasn't done anything to me, Georgie," I said, filling his silence. "But he isn't telling me how to do this better. He isn't telling me a lot of things, it looks like, and I thought those like us were different. I thought being chosen meant we had an inside scoop on more than what we're supposed to be doing in saving souls. I want to know why we're doing it this way."

"Because mortal sin was defeated when our Lord Christ died on the—"

"No," I interrupted, not letting him off easy with that same shit we were fed growing up. "Nobody is saying that Christ dying on the Cross wasn't worthwhile, and nobody is fucking saying that Christ doesn't have the answers. What I, me, want is God to answer is why we're always doing *this*. We free one soul, and somewhere down the road that same demon we kicked out will show up again for some other poor saint to deal with. What's the point?"

"God works in mysterious ways," George said, his tone serious. "We do not ask why, only where. And those people are given a chance to repent and redeem themselves in his eyes."

"But if all things are of God's will and his making, then he led them to Satan in the first place to allow their souls to be corrupted. Genesis 45 doesn't give him a free pass, and he admits to it in Isaiah 45:7. He allows it—not the person, not the demon, and not even Satan himself. Him. God is making these people suffer."

"Isaiah 45:7 is also definite in its statement. What's your point, Patrick?"

"My point is that it sucks. We're fighting Perdition, not healing the world like Christ wanted."

"Christ reminded us not to beat our swords in plowshares," he said, paraphrasing the lines killers usually liked the best.

"And Christ says that all things come to God."

He grabbed one of the Green Spots and brought it to his lips. "So what?"

"So why aren't we trying to save the demons, too?"

George slammed the empty glass on the vinyl after he took the shot better than expected. "Too far."

"When is the idea of doing what Christ told us going too far?"

"When it is blasphemy." George grasped his second glass, his knuckles white.

That first shot I imbibed from my pair flooded my face with heat, my throat with ease, yet I did not utter more words, more arguments. It's impossible to argue worldview when priests beat it into us as children.

At least, for some of us. I think Yeats wouldn't have stayed silent as I finished the second shot.

We ordered two more rounds before we headed off to hustle some demons.

17

TOO MANY COOKS

The sun had long set when the club threw open its doors. Girls in plastic heels and glittering dresses clutched sparkling clutches, shivering from head to toe while hoping their smile and a certain amount of cleavage got them past the two bouncers behind the red velvet line.

George and I took the back alley again, hiding his sword behind one of the dumpsters after some protest. Much to my non-surprise, the kitchen offered an easy way in as it had before, filing us past waiters and heat lamps before braving the already growing lines to the bathrooms. We breezed past the main room where Pitbull bounced around an empty dance floor. A few of the patrons who showed up early to claim tables and couches hovered at the edges, staring at their smartphones.

"It's so loud," George complained as we crossed the hall to the bar. Taking two seats at the counter, I waved off the lass before she came to serve us. The whiskey from the pizzeria still buzzed in my temples.

"Right," I said a few minutes after we settled into our vantage points. From where I sat, I could see the entrance, the hallway to the bathrooms, and as long as nobody rode the brass rails, the VIP section where the demons and I first ran into each other. "Save our seats. I'll be right back."

"Where you going?" George asked, his hand raised for the bartender. He slurred his words.

Wonderful—a drunk Dragonslayer and a lightweight. "I'm going to go bless the sprinkler system, mate. Just in case we need a backup."

"Does that actually work?" he asked, honestly curious.

"I dunno," I said. "Didn't get to use it last time."

"Bloody fucking hell, Patrick."

"Just get some food in you, you whiny git."

I left him to order us a round of beer and whiskeys. My knees and wrists didn't throb like they usually did as I found the red fire box beside the bar. Thankfully, George's loud as a shit ordering covered for my quick cross and prayer routine, blessing the system, pipes and sprinkler heads like that bowl by the altar you always see on Sunday.

George had a beer and two whiskeys ordered for himself, leaving me a shot and a brew for my own company.

"Why are you drinking so much?" I asked when I sat back down next to him.

"I usually don't do this without my sword. I shouldn't have left it in the alley's dumpster."

"You don't exorcise demons without a sword?"

"It's pretty integral to my process," he said, downing a sniff of Jamison.

"You know how fucking weird that sounds, right mate?"

"Oh, fuck you, Shaggy."

Wonderful—a belligerent, drunker Dragonslayer. At least my shot hampered the growing worries in me warning of how this could all go sidewise.

The hours carried as more people rolled in. Cigarette smoke and a small bit of green flavored the air alongside too much cologne and that sugar stink girls buy at malls, thinking they smell like models instead of dirty, dirty strippers. The heat in the room rose with each body that joined the growing dance in the center of the floor. DJs dressed in neon faux-80s swag switched places a few times.

George drank. And drank. And hit on the bartender, who I promised an extra hundred on her tip to make up for it. And he drank some more.

I had seen soldiers do the same thing before battle since the Dark Ages.

I had killed one or two people in this life, and only because I had to. There were beatings, horrible injuries I had inflicted upon others, but not like what George did to the poor bastards the Chair sent him after. The Holy Roman Catholic Church made an honest-to-God saint into a killer in case they needed one. He was better in the worst ways than I ever wanted to be, but that was also the world he had first lived in.

My first life was doing what I did now—a priest and exorcist. Well, at least one of those. George was a knight first. Men who were chosen to kill things in the name of God. He slew a dragon. I wondered often if he felt this exorcism business was beneath him.

I watched the club for the next few hours until midnight rolled around, and for a moment I worried that the demons had gotten smart and knew better than to show up at the same place twice.

Thank God they sauntered in around one.

Decked out in new fishnet whatevers, the twelve-year-old known as Nariel led the way with the blonde Mehmet well insulated in her posse. Half a dozen or so young folk in their teens and twenties flanked her, each and every one of them holding black oblivion in their eyes.

They saw me immediately.

I nudged George and pointed in their direction as they entered the roped off VIP area.

Any sluggishness faded in an instant, his tired eyes steeled to cold, gray clarity. Drawing out our vestments, mine green and his crimson, we laid them about our necks on the march through the crowd. Palming my rosary, I realized I left my Bible back in Jersey.

Oh well. Between George and I, we could have put together the seven original translations and I could do the Mack Daddy in full Irish.

"Oh ho," I called at the top of my lungs when we topped the steps to their private area. "Round Two!"

The demons rose in unison, a few of them pulling hooked karambit knives.

George started, drawing a cross in the air. "Hold, things of Satan, and know that the Lord is among you!"

"Holy shit," I cawed. "The boys are back in town and coming for your butts!"

Nariel's tiny voice screeched out of the possessed child's body. "You're not supposed to come in here! You're not supposed to come in here!"

"And Jesus wasn't welcomed in the temple." I pulled out my green stone rosary like Mick Foley's sock. "And I'm sure those priests didn't like the whip, either."

The next few minutes were a blur covered by the thumping beat of Nicki and Cardi getting into a fight with each other, the stomp and stamp of the crowds on the dance floor.

George disarmed one of them immediately, wrenching the knife from a shattered hand and kicking the poor bastard dead center in the chest.

A quick twist of the wrist wrapped my rosary around my hand, which stung as I belted the closest demon in the face. I put him right on his ass, giving me time to deck the man next to him with a high kick.

"Fucking shut it," George shouted.

The entire fight ended in a lurch. We all turned in his direction to find the Englishman ringing his arm around Nariel's young neck, the curved blade he had taken from the boy pressed to the side of his throat.

"Everyone calm the fuck down," Mehmet said, her face shifted into the snarling visage of a chimera. "Calm down!"

"What the fuck is wrong with you?" one of the demons asked George. "You can't knife a kid!"

"There's a line, dude," added the demon I had put down first, rising easily to shake off my left. His mouth leaked red. "There's just a line."

"Shut the fuck up," George shouted, his outline wreathed in pulsing laser light. Nariel gurgled when he jerked the boy higher, lifting the small body off his feet. The mortal's face turned purple as the husk involuntarily kicked. "Everyone put your shit down on the couches."

"Everyone just do it," Mehmet said, her order answered in a clatter of knife blades and unopened vodka bottles thumping the red couch cushions. "Please don't hurt him."

"Let him down, George," I said, waving at him to do so. "They get the point."

"They're fucking demons," George snarled back at me. His knife hand tensed, pressing the tip of the curved karambit against the carotid artery until Nariel squealed some more. "All they deserve is—"

"Okay, okay, okay," I said, my hands out at all parties. "Let's just take a moment, eh? No need to send someone's host to the morgue."

"Then tell your psycho friend to put the knife down," Mehmet cried.

I point at Mehmet and Nariel. "Everyone out except you two."

George grunted like a bull. "You can't be bloody serious!"

"Oh, fuck this." I hopped on the table like I had days ago, smiling down at Mehmet as she watched me draw out my lighter in confusion. Then memory set in, as did a delicious expression of "oh, shit" on her face. I read Mehmet's lips when the music from the dance floor drowned out her voice.

"Oh, fuck. Alright, everyone out."

There was a bit of unimportant argument between Mehmet and a few of her cohorts before they shuffled out.

When it was just Mehmet, myself, George, and a purpling Nariel, I nodded to the nut job. "Put him on the couch, George."

To his credit, he shoved Nariel on the couch beside Mehmet, where the possessed huffed until normal color returned to his face.

I stepped backward off the table, putting it between us again. Looking from one to the other, I turned the lighter in my fingers over and over. "So, you're all working for a baddie, ain't you?"

The pair stared back, wordless save for the deep rage held within their gaze.

I knew things would have gone badly if I hadn't had my heavy. "One of you needs to talk or I'm not going to stop him," I added, nodding in the direction of a drunk, seething George. He held the knife he had taken from one of Mehmet's goons by his side, the strobe lights flashing green, red, and pink on its four flats. "And you know he doesn't mind what he'll do to the little one."

"Another rape by a priest?" Nariel dared to peep before Mehmet hushed him, setting her hand on his shoulder. "Shocking."

George made a weird noise when the boy said that.

"Look," I said, trying to keep my own tone genial, "neither of you two are walking out of here in those meat suits. I know your names, and more importantly, my friend here doesn't like being called a rapist."

"You're a priest and you tried to knife a little kid?" Mehmet asked the Englishman.

I snapped my fingers and got her attention. "No, no, over here. Back to business. You're not walking out of here, but you don't have to be dragged kicking and screaming back to Perdition if you don't want to. He and I will make this quick, and without violence, if you just answer me one question."

"You barged into our club, threatened us with a knife, all for one question?" Mehmet asked, her head tilted at an odd angle. "You could have just come and asked."

"Weed and head trauma does things to the memory." I held my hands out in defeat. "Now you want this deal, or does my friend here get all dicey?"

My spine crawled when George smirked for effect.

It made its point to the possessed woman. She and Nariel looked at each other and shrugged, accepting their defeat with much less protest than demons had ever given me. "What do you want to know?"

"Where's Thomas Cromwell?" I asked.

"How do you know that name?" Nariel asked, all of his spite and fury gone.

"He didn't say you could ask questions," George rumbled.

"Down, ya bastard," I chided before addressing Nariel. "It doesn't matter how I know that name. What I want to know is where he's at in this city. That's all."

Mehmet sighed and squared her shoulders. "Dennison Tower. He was given a series of apartments by the president."

My rosary, green and pale and old with its silver, weighed in my hand like a cannonball. "Of course he was."

There, and done with duty, the four of us waited in the VIP section while the crowd outside of us sinned, sang, and shook their way through the travails of their weeks, wasted equally on meaningless experiences that wouldn't make up for shit jobs and unhappy relationships the next day.

I envied them. Sometimes normalcy was the greatest temptation.

I stepped onto the table again, flicking alive my lighter until the flame danced, high and thin. Lifting it up to the closest sprinkler, my motion motivated George.

He pulled out his rosary, a long line of black beads fixed together by an old wooden cross. He shoved the coffee table out of the way. "Which one's mine?"

The water kicked on, followed by a fire alarm that blared throughout Bar Rochelle. Several people screamed while everybody rushed the exit, the exact opposite of what every single one of us was taught in school. I was taught by Catholics and those fucks believed in orderly lines. To my own comfort, the water was actually warm like a shower, though the smell of tin and sand infused the wash.

It smelled a bit like old Dublin when the rain washed the shit away, taking the rats with them.

The demons on the couch went rigid.

"Well?" I asked when the club was empty, Rihanna's voice echoing about yellow diamonds in the splatter-spray chamber I had made.

Like prisoners being asked who'd like to die first, they stared glumly at the dirty black floor. George stood guard beside them, hovering with his knife in constant sight.

I glanced at the blade. "Put it away, George. No need to make this harsher than it need be."

Water dripping down his face, George dead-eyed them before he dropped the knife onto the floor.

"I'll go first," Nariel said, his face hidden in his hood. He spoke in a small, wounded voice, like a dog that had been kicked.

I held up my rosary, the silver Irish cross at its end wetted bright. "Nariel, in the name of the lord's mother, Mary, and her son, who died upon the cross for your redemption, flee from this vessel and let the Lord's light clean this soul. Return to darkness in the name of the Father, Son, and the Holy Spirit. Amen."

The boy's body seized for a moment before he fell to the side on the couch, unconscious and soaking into the cushion. George let out a heavy exhale of relief, which I shared.

Not all demons left so kindly.

"Nariel's host was this one's little brother," Mehmet said, bereft of her human voice. "Do not worry about leaving them alone to wake."

"Why would you care?" George asked.

The sprinklers died. Left soggy down to the flesh, I waited for Mehmet to wipe the wet out of her make-up smeared eyes. "Leave it, George."

"What, like you did?" he spat back.

I didn't even address him as I gathered my rosary in my palm and pressed it onto the demon's shoulder. Mehmet flinched but held against the onslaught of the sanctified object. I drew close and whispered in her ear, hoping the music drowned out my words so George couldn't hear. Fuck him and his dogma.

"I beseech thee, Mehmet, to leave this vessel and return to Perdition. God bless and keep you, demon. When you see Mary, don't look away. Please don't look away. Now begone, and let this soul, and yours, wash in the Lord's light. Amen."

For a moment, I thought the demon sobbed before it left the woman's body.

18

———

THE LASS

We used George's black card to buy a night at a four-star in Midtown. We bought separate rooms, so tired of each other he didn't argue over an extra grand for peace and quiet.

The soft light of the lamp next to me glared off the face of my smartphone as I flicked through pictures of last night's reporting from Rome. The Chair still remained missing, the count had risen past fifty, yet the Church held its line to promising services across the world in this time.

Not perfect, but at least they weren't dead.

The screen buzzed.

Merry's name and number emblazoned across the glass.

I tapped the little green dot. "Hiya, Merry."

"Patrick, it's not Merry," Deevi said from the other end, her voice as clear as bell-song. "She drank a lot and fell asleep after you and George left. I took her phone. It's me, Deevi."

"Aye, lass," I said, my head sunk into the pillow. "I know it's you. How could I not?"

She made a happy sound in her throat. "Are you safe?"

"Aye, we are. Holing up for a bit before I call a few friends of mine from back home. We think we might know where that Cromwell is in the city."

"Are you going to save his soul?"

Thankfully, the truth was pliable this time. "In a manner of speaking."

Quiet. One of those weird moments every one of us experienced, the silence on the phone that carried for long, complicated seconds.

"So Merry drank a lot?" I asked.

"A full bottle of the brown stuff she called rum. Talked about a lot of things before she fell on the couch."

One was always curious about voodoo. "Oh?"

"Did you really once exorcise a demon from a porn star and then sleep with her as a reward?" she asked.

God damn it. "I did. Her name was Rachel," I said, compelled to the truth even over the many miles between us. "Telling stories, then, did she?"

"A few," Deevi said, clearly amused. "We talked a lot about sex."

I said nothing.

"She said you like fun girls."

Oh, goddammit. "Did she now?"

"Am I a fun girl, Patrick?" Deevi asked, concerned.

"I don't know."

"You don't know?"

"I don't know if we should be talking about this."

"Why?"

The innocence in her voice, playful and just a hint leading, almost made me grunt like a dog in heat, albeit a frustrated one. "Because it would be inappropriate."

"Why did you stop being a priest?"

The sudden question startled me, but driven on, the words flowed like blood. "Because how can you excuse priests and nuns fucking kids? You don't send them to a different parish, you turn them over to the authorities. We talk about the wrath of God all the time and yet when it comes to our own doing the very worst thing one can do to a child, we back off and 'think of the Church.'" I hated the bitterness in my words. Every single drop. "I was chosen by God to save children, first and foremost, because Christ taught us that they are the way to heaven. 'Do not hinder them', he said, and look what the Church went and did."

"It sounds like you're very angry about it," Deevi said. "Merry said you were angry about it. Are you?"

I made myself not end the call. "I am. And I should be."

"But doesn't God teach us to forgive?"

"He does," I said, "but some things are only forgiven when justice is paid to those who were wronged in the first place. Not everything can be washed away so easily."

"But what about the flock?"

She dragged no truth out of me on that one. "What of…them?"

"What has happened to your church's followers? Have they been wounded? Are they lost?"

"I don't know about them, love. They're—" I bit the inside of my cheek. "Sometimes I look at the people in the world and feel far, far away from them. In my heart I want to save them, I do. But…"

"What troubles you?" she asked, her voice golden honey.

Asked to lay down my burdens and simply be again, tears stung as I tried to blink them away. I fucking hated everything. Everything. I wanted nothing more than to shut up, shut my eyes, and have her hang up when the answer didn't come.

"God chose me, Deevi," I said, whispering it. "And I don't think he ever chose right. Not on anything. But here I am."

"But through God, you've helped many," she said. "You've freed so many from Perdition's torment, who would have been damned to worse ends had you not."

"But they wouldn't have gotten possessed if God hadn't led them there in the first place."

"He works in mysterious ways."

"Can't we go back to talking about sex?"

Her laughter soothed me more than the clean smell of the room, the bed's fresh sheets, and the simple peace of finally being alone. I wished I had laughed then too, but the point of God and his mysteries stuck. She might be a victim of them, and here she was, defending his work to the last when I could not.

Her faith shamed mine.

"Are you there, Patrick?"

"I'm here, love," I said, groggy. The booze from the club still coursed through me, numbing my hands and feet.

"Are you coming back soon?"

"Not to the farmhouse, and you shouldn't stay there."

"We'll leave in the morning, I think. At least that's what Merry said before she passed out."

"That's my Merry," I said. "Pleasure and business together, that one. Plans well for it."

Another bout of quiet. The receiver against my ear, I wedged it between my head and the cream pillow, so I didn't have to keep holding it up. Sleep weighed my eyes.

"Patrick?"

"Yes, dear?"

"What do we do after all this?"

My eyes fluttered open. My mouth was too dry. "I don't rightly know. The Vatican probably doesn't exist anymore and I'm too pale for Syria. Maybe we go back to my house."

"You have a house?"

"Yeah. In Dublin."

"What might we do in Dublin?"

"Oh, all kinds of things," I said, a few of those words lost. "There's this place in Trinity College with this book. I knew a few of the men that wrote it. It's very pretty."

"You'd take me to see a book?" she asked, a bit wilted.

"A pretty book, with a pretty girl, and we can go on a pretty day."

"Goodnight, Patrick," she whispered to me like she was getting away with something.

"Goodnight, angel."

I woke up drooling on the phone.

19

CHARLIE BRONSON

There was a little Irish pub out in Queens that I won't give the name to, but a quick call to some friends of mine from the old neighborhood opened the door to that little pub and all the things inside.

Lined up on gray shelving units set against the old plaster, dozens upon dozens of assault rifles lay out for our inspection, each one matte-black and accompanied by a small piece of instruction on the weapon, like a wine review at the mart. On the next shelf beneath them rested the first rows of pistols set on white towels.

"Didn't expect you to come calling, Saint Patrick, but I'm glad you did. The boys can really use some cheering up in these times," said the young man who had led us to the back, a small, slight youth with a thick brogue from the other side of where I came up on the isle. Dark-haired and balding, he looked at me with as much humility as I thought a man could muster, literally leaning forward in expectation of a good word.

I never got used to the idolizing. "Oh, of course, lad. What's your name, again?"

"John Sullivan, father."

"Ah!" I clapped him on his shoulder. "Like the boxer."

"My ma went to school for American history," John said, bashful. "Can I get you and your friend a pint?"

"Bless you and draw one for yourself," I said, signing the cross over him. He left beaming as I turned to look at George, who stood a few feet ahead, his back to me. I couldn't tell the expression on his smooth face, but when I imagined hard enough the child-like glee that radiated off of him disturbed me.

"Those are Russian-grade AKs," he whispered, awed.

"Oh, hurry up," I said. "And make sure to bring some rope."

George turned on me. "Are you insane?"

I tried hard to keep a straight face. They didn't let boys like George watch a lot of movies. "No, I ain't insane—Charlie Bronson's always got a rope."

"Who is Charlie Bronson?"

"Just go on." I waved him off for the sake of my own sanity. "Day's a wasting."

George wandered off, muttering something before his focus stole away the words. He picked up one of the assault rifles closest to him and pored it over, hefting it in his hands a few times before he pulled the bolt, opening the chamber to something I've never had the slightest interest in learning about. The fact we were here was not a happy point; royals don't deserve to rule if people are freed by God's grace, but I was never one for strapping up to fight the forces of darkness as the first alternative, and neither was Christ.

Nobody was freed of their burdens with a bullet hole.

Young Sullivan returned with three pints of Guinness.

"Oh, you brought me two," I said, taking two of the glasses before he asked why he wasn't serving George. I didn't need him drunk again and armed with bloody machine guns. I took a hearty sip of the first one I grabbed before licking my lips of the malty wonder. "Tell me, Johnny-boy, how goes the Cause?"

"Aye, the Cause..." John Sullivan looked down at his brown loafers, the pale pate of his head gleaming under fluorescent light. "The blow of the Church's transgressions, Saint Patrick... I would not dare to trouble you with these things."

I nudged the young man with my arm. "It's my job, Johnny-boy. The Church did transgress, horrifically, and it motivated me to do much soul searching myself. I can only imagine what it did to men fighting for their home."

"We're gangsters, now, not freedom fighters. Our rights are to money and drugs, not a man's right to be an Irishman 'lone in Irish lands. And we kill each other like gangsters."

He took a long, hard draw of his glass while I studied him, seeing the weight and ache of a warrior beaten by his own war. I had seen many of them among the druids and Romans alike. A taste of brisk evening to wet my tongue, I set one of the glasses down on one of the armory shelves, leaving it for later.

"Do you act like a gangster?" I asked.

John tried hard not to meet my eyes. "I just do what I'm told."

"Aye, but so did Pontius Pilate." I clapped him on the shoulder. "Far be it from me to tell a fighting man how to fight a war. I'm not in that business, but in the end, God will judge us by our choices. So I ask you, John Sullivan, is the Cause about who is real versus who isn't, or is the Cause about Eire?"

"About Eire," said John, brow furrowed. "Saint Patrick?"

"Yes, my son?" I asked before taking a sip of my brew.

"If you ain't a fighting man, then what is he?" he asked, nodding into the armory.

I glanced at George.

The bastard had made his way to the other end of the room, the black duffel beside him stuffed with at least three assault rifles, a grenade launcher wedged in there with boxes of ammo, and a few pineapples. Standing over a display of glittering combat knives, the glow of the lamps illuminating the case highlighted a hard smile.

"Him?" I said. "He's English."

"English!"

"Hey, Patrick? Do you want a knife?" George asked.

"No, thanks, Georgie," I said. "Not looking to kill too many people."

He grunted as if I had disappointed him.

"Did you actually bring an Englishman into my pub to plunder my armory?" John Sullivan asked, more indignant about who had walked in instead of what he'd done.

"You a mobster, Johnny-boy?" I asked.

He gave me a look that I would have laughed at if I didn't know about the ten lads in the bar John Sullivan would've called in, and George was a saint, not fucking Batman. "Aye, I am," he groused before pounding half of his beer.

"If it makes you feel any better, he's going to kill a man named Cromwell."

"Oh, aye?" He held up his glass for a toast. "Cheers, then."

2 0

EL PRESIDENTE

We rolled by Dennison Tower on Fifth Avenue in the middle of the evening, just after all the employees left work to do whatever they did when not working for that baboon. Even then there were too many people for George to walk in loaded for bear, so we stuffed two of his rifles and most of his explosives in his sword bag, which still looked suspect.

"How are we going to get past reception to even see him in the first place?" he asked after we stowed our car in one of the garages near Madison Avenue.

"You still have your collar?"

"Why wouldn't I?"

My hand had to work at the little pocket on the left side of my coat, a little compartment I had sewn in there for some reason. Long and white, it bit into the apple of my throat.

George donned his. "What's our story?"

Sometimes he was sharp. "This bastard is the head of a church—I bet they at least play at ecumenical outreach."

"Ah. So, we're just visiting?"

"Here to drop off a personal gift from the Vatican."

His expression hardened. "Don't you think that will make them wonder?"

Only a few hours sober, my foolishness dawned on me. "Shit, you're right."

He snapped his fingers. "I got it." George nodded toward the corner of Fifty Sixth and Madison, where the light turned red. "Just fall in."

Past the bronzed glass doors of Dennison Tower, the heels of our boots knocked the cream and cinnamon marble before we came to the faux-gold podium with a brass-plated counter.

Not gold. Cheap brass.

"We're here to see the master," George told the crewcut security guard standing before the bank of four elevators, their eyes fixed on each other.

The guard studied George for a second longer than I liked before his hard gaze flicked to the bag hung on his shoulder. A second later he typed on the keyboard in front of his monitor. "Go on up. The master is in Mr. Dennison's penthouse on the sixty-sixth floor in suite six."

I kept my mouth shut until we were inside the elevator filled with wood panels that turned the hue of the overhead lights yellow. "How the hell did you swing that?"

"Perdition has missions and bases just like we do," George said as he unslung the bag from his shoulder. Out came the sword and its belt, which he strapped around his waist before pulling out the first AK. "They need things picked up and dropped off too," he said as he pulled out a magazine and checked the top round.

"And they took the Vatican, so they would expect frequent drop-offs of special items," I said, following him. "So, what's the plan, Rambo?"

"You need to get in and figure that out for yourself, Paddy," he said, stuffing his belt with more magazines for his rifle before strapping it to his chest like he was in Call of Duty. "I'll follow you from here out."

"Are you still drunk?"

He pulled back the bolt on his rifle before picking up his bag. He pulled a silenced pistol out of it next, which he held to the side and at the ready. "Not yet."

The bell dinged at the sixty-sixth floor. The light that struck my face from the foyer nearly blinded me when the brass doors slid open. Gold, gilt in the crown moldings above pearl-pink walls, tables with legs carved from solid carat—finally, some class. Two guards stood before the white doors to the penthouse, their ears hung with white plastic earpieces.

George raised his gun and killed them both, the silencer of his pistol chipping loudly. The bodies dropped to the marble tile, their brains staining the wall behind them in specks.

"What the fuck?" I shouted, literally shoving my entire body into one of the elevator's corners. "You said you'd follow me from here out!"

"I am following you," George said, unflinching. "Go on ahead."

I palmed my eyes. "Just…can you not be you for five minutes?"

"What do you mean?"

Knights. Bloody, blunt knights. "Just don't murder everyone the moment you see them. We don't know how many people are in there and silencers aren't that silent."

George looked at me like I had spoken to him in Mongolian, which he spoke, but I think I painted the picture. I went on, quietly praying to God that there weren't too many guards on the other side of that door, or that they had more guns than George did. A turn of the handle revealed a sitting room built on the cheapest idea of imperial elegance the new and overly rich could extract from an interior decorator on a limited budget, cast in white and rose-pink. Posh furniture, posed like the photographers were coming from the magazine tomorrow to shoot it, sat empty and bare on the cold floor.

We weren't alone in the sitting room.

Thomas Cromwell faced us from behind the mahogany desk where the old cheese sat, his hands flat on the dark surface of the antique. Up close, the man in the golden throne looked different from the one I remembered on the screen of my smartphone. His skin, smooth to the point of being almost pore-less, shaped to a tight skull that made him too handsome, like Bale when he played that other Patrick. His brown hair slicked back without effort to match his perfect Kennedy eyebrows; I couldn't tear my eyes from his.

Widening gyres of darkness stared back. Endless, endless darkness.

A void.

"Gentlemen," Cromwell said in flawless baritone. "I've been expecting you."

"In name of the mother Mary, you will shut your fucking mouth," said George. He had lifted his rifle. The way his shoulders framed for the shot, the narrowness of his stance—something went wrong.

Cromwell rose from the gilded chair in a fluid motion, faster than any human should. "Those bullets are as useless as your sword, boy. As useless as God's word, or the word of any holiness you may claim. If there was a chance I would have spared you, it is gone. Prepare."

"Goddamn, you are charismatic," I said. "Waste him."

Without pause George responded, the barrel of his rifle spitting fire.

Bullets ripped dark, bloody holes in Cromwell's body, a few passing through flesh and bone to crack the bulletproof glass behind him. Unfazed, he stood there while the patron saint of England unloaded, his expression simply peaceful while hunks of flesh exploded out of his back. The short fall of spent copper jackets, tinkling on the marble, filled the silence when the volley ended.

I didn't have to look at George to know his horror matched mine.

Cromwell hadn't flinched once, not even after a cluster in the center of his chest. Taking the tattered bits of his dress jacket, he buttoned what was left of the navy pinstripe lapels together, covering his battered body. Clearing his throat as he straightened his ruined tie, he raised his right hand at George and waved him off.

Like a puppet dragged by its strings through the air, George crashed into the windows at my right.

I stared at my friend, stunned by the display of power.

He lay there on the floor until, as if still guided by Cromwell's unseen hand, drew up from the hard ground and smashed face-first into the glass again.

And again.

And again.

And again.

I couldn't move.

The sound of flesh crushing against unbreakable glass, the sight of George's body hanging at odd angles every time Cromwell's power pulled him back for another drive—I stood like a statue, unable to will myself forward for the horror coursing through me. This possessed man's will broke mine with barely his notice.

"Stop," I screamed when George's face disappeared beneath the torn, awful swelling. I tackled my friend's limp body, trying my best to hold him against the force trying to pummel him into mush. "Stop!"

George drove forward, his open face leaving a streak of blood as his nose broke flat beyond repair. Cromwell pulled him back again, the weight of the form knocking me off my feet.

My arms locked tight to his torso, I held on for dear life. "No! Stop!"

George's face fractured the bulletproof window, dragging me forward. My knees banged on the marble. He felt so limp in my arms.

"Beg," said Cromwell.

"Please! Please," I begged, desperate to find my feet under me. My boots kept slipping every time he jerked forward. "For the love of God, please!"

We both hit the window with the force of a bad car wreck, sending fans of fissure out along the impenetrable pane. My forehead cracked it on the jolt forward, leaving me in a white, painful light.

The preacher's cultured voice rang in my ears. "Try again."

I couldn't feel George anymore, or any life in my arms. He was gone, lost to death or Perdition or whatever he'd be cursed to. I wanted to pray in that moment for his life, or mine, or for a second of clarity just so I could see what happened around me.

"Please." I pushed the word out of my mouth. "Please."

A sudden force took hold of my body. Twisted upright, I floated like a mummy in the air, bound with invisible bandages.

Cromwell faced me as I floated toward him. His face speckled in blood, his black eyes opened wide until our faces touched, nose to nose. That obtuse hatred filled my vision.

"I remember you," he said, sniffing. "You knocked that rock out of my mouth."

I looked into the face of Satan himself and knew my doom.

2 1

SESSION THREE

I t was the most amazing sight in the world, Satan carrying a rock through the sky. And not just any rock, mind, but Cashel Rock. Look it up on Wikipedia. Before they built that big fucking castle on it, the lord of the Hell wanted to drag that hunk of earth back into the depths of Perdition, to do whatever the Devil did with rocks of that size.

I basically slapped it out of his mouth because I got drunk and found him during my walk back from wherever I had been drinking.

I did a lot of drinking with the druids in those days.

I did a lot of drinking in the present day too.

He remembered well.

"My jaw hurt for years after that day," he said, a wicked smile unhinging Thomas Cromwell's jaw so it could stretch unnaturally wide. "Perhaps God is not as good as you had hoped, priest."

"Former," I said, clearing the last stars the window had left in my head and ears. "Former."

Satan laughed, his voice distorting. "I'll get you anyway."

I tried to look away, but no matter how hard I tried to force my head to the side, to simply will myself to do anything, my entire body locked. Thankful for that one time some of those Italian Satanist buried me alive, I was able to steady my heart alongside my breath the best I could, saving me from a certain heart attack.

"Where is she?"

"Far from here." My mind settled in a suddenness I had not made for myself. The calm disturbed me as much as it put me at ease.

He's just a demon. A fallen angel like the rest. A shadow appeared behind Satan, over his left shoulder. *There's no reason to fear.*

"What are you looking at?" the Devil asked, turning his gross head. He looked right at the apparition standing behind him, then back at me, confused. "Are you maddened now, priest? Have I enacted enough torture already on the barest touch?"

The voice in the depths of my consciousness whispered like it had amused itself.

I struggled. What was this voice in my head?

The shadow leered at me for a second, as if taken aback by the mere thought I had made to question its presence.

Satan grabbed my face, holding my jaw so hard I thought he'd break it. The pressure made my teeth hurt as if they shifted in my gums. "My patience wears."

Torn between the two powers battling for my attention, my brain felt like it was on acid, racing and cooking at the same time. I couldn't hear if George breathed or not. All I heard in my ears was a note.

A single clear note, as if sung by an angel.

Deevi flashed somewhere in me, a spot of comfort I tried so hard to latch onto before it ripped away without warning, hustled onward by the shadow that made this glorious tone. Any levity the voice contained vanished.

Now we go to work, saint.

My hand rose without thought or intention, grasping Satan by his husk's throat. Freed of his unseen will, I raged forward, unable to stop myself as I turned and shoved Cromwell into the fractured window he had broken with George's body.

He struggled against my sudden infusion of unnatural strength, grunting in surprise. "How," Satan asked, his voice rising to the point it sounded like flies buzzing on rotted food. "How are you doing this?"

The shadow stood beside me in my mind's eye, holding up its hand, its fingers curled together around an invisible neck. Realizing this apparition controlled me, even from the outside, a clarion call broke through.

Somehow, I had become possessed by a demon, or at least some being akin to one.

And one more powerful than the Devil.

Fixing him against the bulletproof glass, the entity within me drew us together again, enough so I could smell the mints Satan must have been sucking on before George and I barged in. Words flowed from my mouth that weren't mine.

"The same way I always do it, you dumb goat," I said, my voice used by the shadow's will. My cheeks bunched in a cruel grin. "I'm always better."

A ghost of recognition twisted Satan's human face before it turned to something I never expected to see in the face of any demon, let alone the Lord of Perdition:

Terror.

"No," he said in a half-whine, half-growl. "Not you. Not you. Not now!"

My body backhanded the bastard flush, sending him reeling across the penthouse office and into the dark mahogany desk. Surging, my possessed body swung my foot out in a low-kick when I caught up to him, sweeping Satan off his feet. He landed on the marble floors with a thud, back first, before immediately popping up, angrier than before.

I kicked his feet out from under him a second time, summoning another issue of curses. The spirit possessing me laughed like a child.

"Stop. Just stop," it said in my voice.

Satan rose to his feet in a third attempt, only to be put down by a hard left to the jaw. I felt every bit of.

"Stay down, goat."

Up he came again, and a second left cross buckled his legs. He reeled, no longer eager to assault.

"Stay down, goat," my mouth said, harsher this time in my brogue.

The Devil could have been a contender. A third left put him flat on his back.

"Stay down, you stubborn, dirty, worthless little goat," the demon said, colder, stooping low at an impossible angle to sneer in Satan's dead skin mask. "Don't make me remind you."

"You'll! Never! Beat! Me!" Satan choked at him, each word a shotgun blast of buzzing bees in a barrel full of monkeys. The bastard didn't listen.

The demon kicked my shin into Cromwell's torn face, knocking the husk out completely, if the filth within me hadn't killed the poor man being held by his foe. It ran its fingers through my hair and walked around the desk, taking the time to fix my coat. Everything that was me, that remained, cried to look in George's direction.

No matter how much I tried, I could not bring my tiny, minute speck of existence to pray for him. *Please*, I thought—*just don't leave him there to die.* George was a lost, tortured little boy who never got a chance. Please don't leave him.

Apparently, this demon paid attention. "Agreed, saint," the demon said in my voice. "He has been a useful soldier. Better than most angels."

To my disgust, it glanced toward Satan's prone form. Blood pooled out of Cromwell's broken, pulped face, draining along the seams in the pink marble squares to soak the feet of a gold-plated chair.

The demon returned its attention to George, striding over in a gait that made my bones feel out of place. He knelt down and pressed a finger to his mutilated brow.

George awoke with a gasp, his square face restored to its original state without a sign of damage. "Patrick?"

"Get up, boyo," the demon said in my voice, imitating me down to the long tick of the 'o'. The next few moments disappeared in a few flashes of light.

I woke from the glare to find George knelt in the middle of the elevator floor, working at something in his bag of guns.

"You almost done?" the demon asked.

"Keep your fucking shirt on," he said, pressing down on a lever attached to a wired box before he zipped up the bag. Lifting a modded-out M4 and feeding it a fresh magazine, he faced me with a resolute nod, no worse for wear than when we walked in. "We have ten minutes."

"For what?" the demon asked, honestly curious.

George eyed me oddly.

The ride down the elevator went without incident on the way to the third floor, where we took the stairs to a service exit.

"You all right?" George asked me when we cleared the alley after we ditched his gear in the dumpsters.

"Yeah, fine," said the demon.

They crossed the street, marching a few blocks down Fifth Avenue until a loud explosion rocked the New York skyline. Dennison Tower's top floor blazed, smoking a column of black that would be seen for miles. Every single person on the street shouted, stopped, save for George and my possessed body, which marched on through.

Patience, saint. Patience.

CONFESSION

"I can't believe you blew up Dennison Tower," Merry said, her voice faraway but loud. "You're lucky nobody caught you."

"Took care of the problem, didn't it? And it was only the top few floors," George said in a bored tone. "And I don't hear you rushing to offer anything better."

"When will Patrick wake up?" Deevi asked in the kitchen.

Her voice opened my eyes, and it was me who opened them to look out into the living room of the Jersey farmhouse. Someone had laid a fleece blanket over me, the soft fabric heating my bare chest and gathering sweat. Blinking a few times, I opened and closed my hands before I started on the couch, bolting right up.

Deevi's golden wings poked through the kitchen's doorway.

I tried to swallow my panic, failing to control the heave of my chest. My boots and coat lay on the wooden floor beside me, discarded as if I had simply taken them off and left them there like a normal, non-possessed person. My memories of everything after the explosion seemed garbled in my own mind.

Stay calm.

The demon's voice in my head made me scream involuntarily.

Deevi rushed into the room. "Patrick! What's wrong?"

"I'm possessed!" I screamed at her, spasming off the couch as the truth broke me. I felt in control of my body, but not, as if the tingle under my skin would erupt into creeping, crawling ants at any moment, unable to stop myself from whatever this malevolence would desire to do.

The mere sight of Deevi in the room heightened my panic.

George and Merry rushed in behind her.

"Patrick, calm down! You're safe," Merry said, a hand out in hopes that I would stop myself.

They wouldn't understand. The way George looked at me, he knew. His hand crept near his pocket.

He had a gun. He would have gone for the gun first.

I saw the bay window overlooking the dead cornfields outside.

Don't you dare.

I ran headfirst through the panes the moment the demon spoke, landing hard on the brown grass amid the raining, glittery shards. The cold made my muscles seize when I crawled to my feet, darting toward the field, the trees, wherever I needed to go so I wouldn't hurt my friends.

A quarter-mile passed before tears filled my eyes. My bloody feet, torn and shredded by the frozen cornstalks littering the heath, tripped over themselves. I landed hard in the cold dirt, my face pressed to the gritty soil.

"Crawl," I screamed at myself. My body refused. "Crawl away!"

No.

"Please," I begged. More tears. My entire body was racked as I tried to grind it into the farm field. "Please don't go back. Please don't hurt her."

Why do you think I would hurt her?

Pushing up to my hands and knees, I kept crawling. The debris in the dirt tore at the tops of my feet and toes, my palms, but I shoved past the pain. Fuck the pain.

Fuck God.

How could God have done this to me?

Demons can only take hold of a mortal soul with his permission.

Why me?

I would have owned up to my sins.

Who said you sinned?

Roaring through the alien question, my crawl zapped the last bit of life from me. Hot, hard desperation brought me forward until sheer exhaustion threatened my erratic, chasing heart.

Her winged shadow fell over me.

I stopped, weeping like a damn prisoner who had failed his escape.

I had failed. Oh God, I had failed.

The cuts on my feet covered my toes in blood, the sear of their torture causing me to curl my body inward like a wounded animal. Still bare from the waist up, the sharp tines of black husks stabbed my side before the cold wind of the Jersey winter stole more of my air.

Deevi whispered to me, gentle and sweet. "Patrick?"

I rocked in the dirt, sobbing like a madman. I jerked in her hands as she touched me, so ashamed that she had sullied herself upon my unworthiness.

She didn't deserve to be shackled to me.

"Patrick." Her forehead against my cheek, she raised me up in her arms like she was the Madonna. "It's all right. It's going to be all right."

"I'm possessed," I choked into her brown locks, which had fallen over my face and obscured the winter sun. "Get away. You need to get away."

Her lips moved against my temple. "I'm not going anywhere."

George shouted from far away, the footfalls of his boots cracking the frozen soil. "Patrick! Patrick!"

"Keep him away," I whispered to her. "He'll want to kill me. I know he will. I'm possessed."

"Shush," she said, breaking her face away from mine to look at George and Merry as they charged over. "What's that in your hand, George?"

I braced, knowing he had brought his sword. They'd fight, she would kill him, and the demon would get one more.

"First-Aid Kit," he said, compelled by her power to the truth. "I need to take care of his feet."

"What happened?" Merry dropped to her knees in front of my face. She forced my clenched eyes open with her fingers. "Tater? Where are you?"

Tell them.

"I'm here," I cried, almost groaning the words. "It's telling me to speak!"

"Speak what?" Merry asked, confused but gentle.

"I don't know!" I howled. "I don't know!"

"All right, all right," Deevi said, in my ear again. "What is the demon's name?"

Should you tell her?

I sobbed, shaking my head in one last attempt to fight my way free of Deevi, of my friends, of the world. I needed to run as far as I could, until this voice, this proud, assured, clear voice could no longer have cause to speak, or harm.

"I don't know," I jabbered. "I don't know. I don't know. I don't know..."

Deevi and Merry cradled me together as I wept and blubbered. I yelped when George poured alcohol over my feet, holding the right one still in his hand.

You ungrateful mortal. I brought you along to find Deevi, set you on the path to Cromwell, and saved your bits of mud and clay when I could have simply blown up that heathen temple myself. I could have cared not a moment whether the Dragonslayer lived or died, as it is your duty. You know who I am.

"No!" I thrashed again. "No!" The demon was trying to tempt me, to surrender to honeyed words that would carry me further toward Perdition.

I decide on Perdition.

"It's an archdemon!" I sat up and looked right at George before terror forced me into unconsciousness, too strained by my mania. "An archdemon!"

I thought, before the world died away, the knight nodded back at me.

2 3

SESSION FOUR

I woke in the barn tied to a chair.

My feet bandaged with enough wrap that they didn't touch the ground for the layers of gauze, I could feel the morphine coursing through me, leaving my entire body dulled to the point where I wasn't going any-fucking-where.

But I felt the demon in the back of my mind.

Knowing something is there is sometimes worse than the ignorance of its presence—that's where I usually came in to help people through. Sometimes spotting a demon is easy. Sometimes it started with coughing. Long, constant coughing, before suddenly your voice sounded different enough that something else felt different.

I smoked so much so how would I know?

Then one day you cough out a black nail that you never swallowed. Anthony Hopkins was not far-off, bless him.

Children were often the hardest to diagnose with possession before the nail showed. They were both living in a realm of magical thinking that manifested directly from their young subconsciousness and the experiences life had handed them so far. A psychologist often came in first, and I knew many.

I don't know where or when I felt different. Perhaps after the lwas? Multiple cultures around the world believe that the psychedelic as well as the ecstatic experiences opened one to outside forces beyond the mortal realms. Perhaps it snuck in when I was blitzed out talking to West African spirits.

No, not then.

"Shut up," I spat, my breath fogging the chill air in the barn.

The padlock on the doors popped free. The barn entrance slid open to the late-afternoon light.

George entered first, dressed in his blacks. His red vestments hung around his neck. Coiled in one hand, his Syrian rosary looked like drops of blood that had failed to fall, caught by God's grace and arranged in beauty.

You Catholics are a morbid set.

He held a plastic bottle of holy water in the other.

Deevi and Merry followed behind him, dressed in sweats. Merry gripped a syringe which she tried to hide behind her back.

"Was that?" I asked, nodding at it.

"More morphine. Not enough to kill you," said George. "Look at me, Patrick."

I looked up at him. A five o'clock shadow on his handsome face, his eyes fixed mine.

"Repeat the Lord's Prayer with me," he whispered. "Follow along."

"Our Father," we intoned together, like boys back in the rectory. "Who art in Heaven, hallowed be thy name, thy kingdom come, thy will be done on earth as it is in heaven. Give us this day our daily bread and forgive us for our trespasses as we forgive those who trespass against us and lead us not into temptation but deliver us from evil."

Here it came.

"For thine is the kingdom, the power, and the—"

"Finish it," said George.

"No," I said. Was that me?

"Finish it."

"I can't."

"Do you hear it speaking?" he asked. "Is the demon telling you not to speak, Patrick?"

"No, he just won't let me fucking say that part!"

"Oh, fuck it." George unscrewed the top of his holy water bottle and slashed it in front of him. Water splashed my face and chest, blinding me for a moment and making me snort when some of it got in my nose. Shivering, I shook my head to get the wet off me.

"Come out, demon," George intoned, jabbing his rosary into my forehead.

The simple cross hurt like a motherfucker, snapping my head back. "Ow, you fucking dolt!"

He looked down at me, anger mixing confusion. "Why aren't you boiling?"

"Because I'm not," I said up at him. "Is this your first go?"

Merry appeared at George's side. "You're not going to get anywhere beating him up, you damned thug. Watch me get through to him." The Vodun priestess grabbed my face like she had so many times before. "Tater, is the demon talking to you?"

There was my girl. "Not unless it wants to."

Almost pushed out of the way, George leaned down into my sight. "Is it tempting you?"

"No more than I already am," I said. "I saw shadows at first, snatches of movement, and felt this urge to find Deevi. And once I found her, the urge went away, and all I felt—"

The demon didn't stop me this time.

I did.

"What did you feel, Tater?" Merry asked, stilling holding my face.

I knew this moment would come, when the lwas told me she and I wouldn't be what we were after. Like death flashing before my eyes, I remembered meeting a young girl in Haiti that lured me in and never let me go, and I never wanted to. She and I had been through so many adventures, so many things.

I had loved this woman like a wife. I knew I had loved her the moment the Chair sent me to her hut, looking for me to do what they raised me to do against witches, sorcerers, and those who conjured.

Now we looked at each other, knowing in our hearts what I would say.

Tears burned my eyes. "I love her, Merry. I don't know why, but I do. I love her more than you, or Christ, or God. I love her more than I love Eire."

There was always this weird moment, I found, where tears actually sharpened all things. I saw the diamonds in her eyes as well, brimming like a coming wave on her long, black lashes.

Merry swallowed. "Then what happened?"

"It possessed me in Dennison's office, when George and I went to find Cromwell. It let me go after we escaped. He's only talked a little since." I shivered in the chair, still wet from the water.

Merry searched the barn. "We need to get him a blanket."

"We're not done here," said George, holding his Bible to his chest. "Not until this is taken care of."

Merry turned on him. "So you're going to let him freeze? It's fucking Jersey!"

"Here."

Like the arrival of the grace I desperately needed, my angel appeared, my coat in her hand. Her wings glowed soft in the shadows of the barn, their light a lantern of hope. Deevi put my peacoat around my bare shoulders, pulling the lapels together before placing her hand in the center of my sternum.

"Patrick, will you teach me how to say the Hail Mary?" she asked. "The monks used to chant it in their cells, and I would like to hear you say it."

"Hail Mary, full of grace…" The words came out of my mouth quicker than whiskey, and I laughed for a moment.

I got you, you dumb motherfucker.

Have you?

"The Lord is with thee." I'm only one step behind. "Blessed thou are among women and blessed is the fruit of thy womb, Jesus. Holy

Mother of God, pray for us sinners, now and at the hour of our death. Amen."

What did you try to prove there? That I hate women and babies?

"Well, do you?" Deevi pressed her hand to my chest. "Do you hate women and babies?"

"Who are you talking to?" Merry asked the Nephilim, letting go of me.

"You can hear it," I said, freed to face the one who had taken my heart. "You can hear—"

My tongue swelled immediately in my mouth, cutting off my breath in a choke.

Silence.

Deevi surged forward, lifting me out of the chair with one hand. Dangling like a ragdoll, she pressed me against the corrugated steel wall of the barn. Pinned like a butterfly, she grabbed my face with her other hand in a skull-crushing grip. Her golden eyes became all I saw.

"You will let him speak!" she cried, the light of her wings flaring to a shimmering white.

I watched helplessly as the Nephilim's searing golden eyes stared into me, unable to shirk or break the bond she had made with a hand on my heart, latched to my soul. My mouth somehow worked on its own as my tongue deflated. Air rushed into my body, and I gasped so hard that not even the pressure of Deevi's strength stopped my chest from expanding.

They are watching.

"I demand you reveal your name, demon!" She screamed in my face in Aramaic, a lion's roar that dropped both Merry and George to their knees and clapping their ears in panic. The intensity of her wings strengthened, like a nova gone awry.

Allowed to breathe, I let myself slide into unconsciousness against the wall where she held me, the chill of the metal numbing every inch of my body. I didn't care if I shivered or even died in that moment. I just wanted this to stop.

Please God, make it stop.

Please.

Willed by her might, Deevi's wings dimmed. Hugging me to her chest, she took me from the wall and carried me like a babe to the concrete. She held me like Magdalene did when the Lord came off the cross, and I let myself fall into the warmth of her arms.

She held my face, never breaking eye contact with me. "Leave him be."

Then bring me a chicken.

BOCK-BOCK-BOCK

We sat there while George and Merry disappeared, exiting the barn in search of the required fowl in the coops behind the building. Laying in Deevi's arms, one of them had laid another blanket over me, a continued kindness I'd remember for the rest of my days. She rested against the wall, holding me still as she watched the crack of the door. Somewhere the light was ebbing on the earth, twilight's last feathering between day and night.

I tried to speak, my throat parched. "Dee-vi?"

She broke her gaze away from the door, her placid expression replaced by a warm, true smile as she looked down upon me. "Yes, Patrick?"

"Please don't leave me."

"Oh, I won't." Her smile wavered.

I tried to swallow some moisture. "What?"

"What?" she asked, restoring her happiness.

"You're sad."

This time any attempt at joy vanished. "I'm angry at the Lord for the moment."

Maybe it was the old priest in me, or the evangelist that walked the entire breadth of Ireland, but sorrow rose. "Why?" I replied, trying and failing to ease the shivers that racked my body. I left my mouth open, so my teeth didn't chatter.

Using her free hand, Deevi tucked the blanket tighter around my body. "Nothing is done without God's hand. His hand was in this."

As it is in all things.

The barn door swung open again. George held it open while Merry scuttled in, hushing and cooing at an old brown hen that clucked, clearly disturbed by the energy in the room. Animals were good for picking out stuff like that.

I want a rooster.

Deevi grumbled and sighed. "It wants a rooster, Merry."

Merry stopped dead in her tracks, sharing an insulted expression with George.

"Do you know how long it took me to chase down this fucking bird?" George asked, pointing at the hen, who responded by clucking in confusion.

"You ran after chickens until I called one to you," Merry said with a snap. "And I don't give a good goddamn if the demon wants a rooster."

"Well, I don't think it is going to leave until it gets a rooster," Deevi said, like there was no other option in the world.

"I'm not chasing a cock for any demon," George declared.

The hen clucked some more at that.

"Holy shit, just get the rooster so I can get this demon out of me," I begged, tired of the chicken's noise already. "Please? Can we focus on that?"

To my surprise, he left without a moment's argument, with Merry following after she side-eyed me for the sass. I'd hear about it at some point.

They both returned after I had found the peace of a small nap in Deevi's arms.

"Get in, you rank bastard," George said, throwing a brown-green rooster into the barn. The proud bird flapped his gauzy wings before landing perfectly upright, his bright red comb and wattles on full display as if no one had just manhandled him. Brown at the head, his hackle was the most particular shade of blue before his cape and the rest of his body transitioned to a dark green color. The tail feathers, assorted slashes of black, red, and brown, puffed in smooth sickles.

That will do.

"Now leave him," Deevi ordered the thing inside of me.

At first I felt nothing, but then this sudden unease came over me, like bad sausages from the pub. It passed as quickly as it arrived, my stomach gurgling a few seconds before my entire body settled back into the hunger, the thirst, and the searing pain of my hands and feet. Suddenly aware of my wounds because of my freedom, I stifled a cry that crept behind my face and settled there for a few minutes.

"I don't feel any different," I told Deevi.

"Were you expecting Mary?" asked the rooster.

We all lost our collective shit.

"That fucking chicken's talking!" George pulled out his Bible and held it in front of him and Merry like a shield. "I've never seen a fucking demon talk through an animal, Patrick!"

"Why do you keep assuming that?" the rooster questioned, turning completely around to face the Englishman with his tail feathers up. "You keep assuming that."

I rolled out of Deevi's lap and onto my wrapped feet. Without rosary, the Good Book, my vestment, holy water, or even a baseball bat I could use to smash the fucking bird if he got out of hand, I steadied my breath the way the warriors back in the convent had taught me to do as a young child soldier. Some of those tricks were useful.

I rattled one off, spitting it out loud so I could hear it in my actual ears.

"Our Father, who art in Heaven, hallowed be thy name, thy kingdom come, thy will be done, on earth as it is in Heaven. Give us this day our daily bread, and forgive us for our trespasses, as we forgive those who trespass against us. Lead me not to temptation but deliver me from evil. For thine is the kingdom, the power, and the glory, forever and ever. Amen."

"Better?" The rooster pecked in my direction. "Now that is out of the way, we must escape. They are coming."

"Who?" I asked. "Who is coming? Who are you?"

"There's no time," the rooster cried in his shrill voice. "We must away! Away, I command!"

"You're a fucking chicken! Who are you commanding?" Merry shouted, stomping over to him. For a Vodun priestess, the expression on her face teetered between awe and downright indignation. When they're food and sacrificial animals, a lot of prideful things come up, I guess.

A horn sounded outside the barn—loud, deep, and echoing.

Raphael's horn.

My heart almost stopped.

Deevi went to the barn doors first, her flaming sword appearing in her right hand like molten bubbles forming from thin air, shaping themselves into the curved edge, guard, and hilt that wrapped completely around her hand. She nearly moved George to the side to open the portal the rest of the way, revealing the farmstead in its cold, rotted fallow.

Until I looked at the sky.

The clouds churned in a counter-clockwise circle, the sun forming the corona of a white-hot hole. Thunderclouds flashed without noise.

Seven figures descended from the light, carried upon wings of pure, perfect white. The being at the point of their geese-like formation carried a celestial sword of his own, which swirled with the rainbow clusters of nebulas long dead or dying.

"So comes the heavenly host, my kin," the rooster said like he was something out of *Hamlet*, his wattles shaking in triumph. Like a missile he ran for the exit, his neck puffed in an emerald mane of defiance. "My rebellion starts anew!"

"Rebellion?" George called after the charging fowl.

Merry came next, like a domino. "Kin?"

And then Deevi said the word that should have claimed my ghost. "Father?"

I had set loose Lucifer upon the world.

As a rooster.

"Oh fuck," I whispered, palming half my face.

I had talked to his daughter about rubbers and Dr. Dre.

I had gotten my boots on and my arms in the ruined sleeves of my peacoat when the next blast from Raphael's horn sent me to my bruised knees. Writhing on my side amid the drone-screech, an impossible sound not meant to be heard in this world yet, my stomach twisted in knots. The smell of hay, chicken shit, and death mingled in a new, nauseating stench. The rough soil beneath my palms trembled.

Michael the Protector's voice boomed. "You violate your mandate yet again, brother! Does your spite have no end?"

Great. They all talked like Shakespeare.

2 5

HOLY SHIT, BATMAN! ARCHANGELS!

On elbows and knees, I dragged myself across the ground like a snake, the earth tearing at my belly. The gauze bandages around my feet and ankles protected my wounds, but the pain of pulling them through the dirt did nothing to deter the sharpness. I hauled myself to the edge of the barn's doorway.

For some reason, George and I had decided to crawl toward absolute danger because we're idiots.

"Do not try to spoil us with your lies," Michael said, as if in reply. "Your nature is as it is! You are born to spurn the Creator."

My hand fell on the heel of a shoe. Squeezing with all my might, I felt George buck against me for a moment before I tapped on his calf. He thankfully understood before he mule-kicked me in the face. His leg slid out of my grasp, and like the knight he always was, went on ahead into battle as my shield.

Please, Lord. You won't spare me but spare him.

Past the barn door, the light of the archangels' wings blotted out the world. No matter how hard I clenched my eyes, the light snaked in, turning everything white.

I could hear George ahead of me, growling like a damned, defiant dog. Did God think so little of us that he had to be treated like that?

I had to follow George. I had to.

"When the time comes for Judgment, it will be the time, and nothing of the earth or Perdition can alter that," said Michael. "You are lying again, Lucifer."

To my surprise, my hearing slowly returned.

"...time for Judgment is time for Judgment. Shaytan located my daughter, which God assured me he could not, and speak one of you against me! 'He never can or will', and then I find out she was abducted to New York City, of all these loathsome places. Ask him this: father to father, would he do any less? But then I would tell you how they treated him first before he died for these apes. Remember how you cried, Michael?"

"You would—" Michael stopped himself. "We sit at the Lord's feet, not stand at his side. Remember that truth and your place in it."

"I am no more at God's feet than I am at his side," said Lucifer. "And I am standing where I shall stand. Who will move me?"

Deevi spoke up, somewhere in the lighted void. "May I speak?"

"No, abomination, you may not," said Michael.

A fourth voice joined the divine spat, a pleasant resonance. "Michael, she's our niece," whispered Gabriel the Messenger.

"She is an abomination," Michael stated, every word coated with hate.

"She is my daughter," said Lucifer. "And unlike our father, I won't let her suffer for the sake of vanity. Neither his nor Shaytan's."

"May I speak?" Deevi asked again, lacking any of her usual kindness.

"No, abomination, you may—"

"I would like to hear you speak, Deevi," said Gabriel, interrupting Michael.

"First I need you to dim your wings. You are scaring my friends," Deevi said. "And God should scare none."

"You would dare speak to me about God?" Michael questioned.

"Put down that sword and I'll say a lot of things to you about God, brother," said Lucifer. "Dare me before you dare her."

"Stop it, Father," said Deevi. "Stop this, all of you!"

"Dim your wings," called Gabriel. "But first let us put our swords away. We do not need them to speak."

Michael protested like a whining teenager. "But Gabriel, he's not supposed to be here!"

"Are you still whining like that?" Lucifer piped in. "After all these eons?"

"Swords down," Gabriel the Messenger ordered, not asking this time. "Yours as well, Deevi."

"I'd like nothing more," she replied.

As the sound of Raphael's horn faded with the light of the seven archangels, the white blindness receded, and I could look again upon the world. George had crawled a few feet in front of me before he had collapsed from the strain, face down in the dirt. I tried to find Merry, but she had stayed behind in the barn, probably impacted by it all as well.

How I stayed conscious, only God could tell. The second I tried to move my body, without warning, a great groan of agony escaped my lips. On my stomach, and the right side of my face scratched raw by the ground, the sensation of surviving a blast of Raphael's horn wracked me worse than my wounds hoped to muster.

I screamed.

I screamed so loud I thought my eardrums went, crackling, but nothing I had in me withstood the misery of my flesh. My spirit clawed at my bones in a desperate fight to remain united, to stay within the mortal realm, to not be torn to the next place.

Through the torture, I felt Gabriel's light lay upon me, gentle and warm like a summer wind on the bright hills. Their hand touched upon my back, and a rush of air forced its way into my lungs, which I took too hard. Glorious coughing immobilized me once again. They knelt down beside me. Their palm scalded my flesh, but in the way a hot shower scalded when you desperately needed it, or the burn of a good drink on a bad night.

All my pains, my wounds, ended in an instant.

"Hello again, Saint Patrick," they whispered in my ear. "You're having quite the adventure."

Touched by a genuine archangel, I spoke with the fullness of health. "Some not of my choosing."

Gabriel laughed lightly. "Fair. Few rarely are."

"We are not here for a reunion," Michael said. "If we are to speak, then let us speak quickly. Mortals will detect our presence after too long. Their satellites are already moving."

"God did not meet his end of our deal," Lucifer replied. "By our agreement, I was to have custody of my daughter if his stewardship ever failed, to see and raise her as I see fit from now on."

"She is an abomination," Michael spat back.

The rooster dared to step forward. "Call her that one more time."

I posted on my healed hands and knees. "Excuse me."

"Oh, Patrick, please don't," Gabriel said, rising with me. "Remember who holds the swords."

"Oh, come off it, Gabby—Deevi has one, too." On my feet, I finally laid eyes on them. "Would Christ fear swords?"

A full two heads taller than me, archangel Gabriel gazed down upon me with golden eyes, fiery pink hair fluttering out from a handsome face. Their wings, long, flowing, yet angular, hummed with a blue light. The golden robes of shimmering cloth they wore glowed in scintillating colors.

Their six siblings stood side by side, arrayed in their glory.

Michael stood at the front, wielding the Sword of Truth, while Raphael leaned on his massive instrument, the slight teen bearing the giant silver horn that would count off the world's final days with every blast.

Then came Uriel, whose black light gleamed gray and cool off the metal faces of Selaphiel's golden censer, from which he wafted perfect white smoke. Raguel, a little old rabbi even in all his raiment, thumbed through his Book of Law while Michael worked his gob.

Ramiel waved at me when I saw him, which always scared the fuck out of me when one considered he had to make everything Raguel would say in Lucifer or Michael's defense make sense.

Thank God not everybody wanted to talk that day, as Michael and Lucifer did enough for everyone present.

The commander of God's armies squared off with a chicken.

"Pass onward and let myself and my daughter go, Michael," said Lucifer. "This is the last time I will consider you."

The shining point of Michael's sword flicked up from the ground. "She stays with us."

I had had it. "Oh fuck you, Michael!"

There should have been the sound of nails on a chalkboard, or the needle breaking on a vinyl. Every celestial on the field turned in my direction, save Gabriel, who was already shaking their head.

"Last 'fuck'," they whispered. "Please let that be the last 'fuck'."

"No," I said. "I've been beaten up, dragged around, forced to crawl on my belly, my clothes are ruined, and you—" I pointed hard at them first and then at the bird, "—let him in me."

Silence held the field.

"I don't understand your ire, saint," said the rooster. "God allowed me to possess your soul."

I nearly laughed aloud. "You..." I teetered between cursing and sobbing.

"What a vile experience it must have been," Michael muttered.

"Shut up," Lucifer shot back. "At least He takes time to actually speak to me. Have you even been answered yet?"

"You are fallen," Michael shouted back, shaking his blade. "You're fallen! Not me! You!"

"Standing right here," said Lucifer, spreading his wings open in challenge. "Take the first step down brother. I've been waiting."

"Will you both shut up and listen to her." I trained my anger on Lucifer first. "You! Just because God said so doesn't mean I said so. He could have..." My breath caught in my chest, at the end of the silent scream none but God heard. "Someone could have told me. I deserved that." George still lay ahead of me. "He deserved better than that."

Gabriel broke in. "Patrick, if you will listen—"

"You could have told me," I shouted in Gabriel's face. "Now, we're going to listen to Deevi. We all agreed that she gets to speak. Talk, Deevi."

"Now?" Deevi asked.

"Now," I said.

"Right," she began, putting on her best poker face, which wasn't much more than her honest expression. "I'm not going with my father or with you, Michael. I will go with Patrick, George, and Merry, and we will leave. But I am not going anywhere I do not want to."

"Fucking right," I added.

If a rooster could make a sighing sound, Lucifer puffed one out. "Deevi, you must listen to me—"

"No, I don't," she said. "Everyone has been trying to take me from one place to another, and only my friends have been there to keep those people away from me. Only Patrick has been there."

"I possessed Patrick and led him along the path to find you," Lucifer replied, like he spoke to a child. "I'm the reason you were rescued. He's just been trying to keep himself from breeding with you, at best."

"You son of a bitch!" With my best Messi, I sprinted on my restored feet at that little fucking chicken-shit and swung my foot right at his shitty little fucking face. He flapped and dodged the first one but clucked in panic when I brought my other foot around and caught him in his shitty little breast. Beating his wings, he flew out of reach.

Michael howled with mean laughter.

"Stop it," Deevi shouted. Her golden wings, more feathered and natural looking than her forebearers, strobed a golden light. It did not blind or pain, but I found myself back on my hands and knees, struggling to lift myself up.

So were the archangels.

Every one of them had gone down, dropping their implements as their wings flapped in panic. Gabriel grunted an inhuman sound as they tried to push off the earth beside me, weighed against an invisible force. Not far from me, Michael struggled to reach for the Sword of Truth, which had fallen inches from his grasp.

Lucifer clucked like a rooster, pecking uncontrollably at the ground.

"Get up, Patrick," Deevi called to me, and the gravity vanished.

Rising to my feet with no more effort than usual, I stood there for a moment, stunned into absolute silence.

I heard Merry call from behind me. "Tater?" The barn door's hinges creaked. "Oh, by the goddess…"

Before I turned, I spotted Michael lift his golden hand in the priestess's direction. "Watch—"

The archangels blinked out of existence with Merry and George.

The rooster sighed loudly. "That was expected."

26

TEAM ROOSTER

The screen door to the house slammed shut. Deevi had already gone in ahead of me, and to my surprise, picked up the bottle of whiskey. She sought something near the sink.

Lucifer pecked the other side of the screen door after I shut it behind me. "Let me in, saint."

"Did you hear something, Deevi?" I asked. "I swear I heard something."

"You act the child yet again," the rooster said.

Deevi washed out a glass and poured me a finger of Green Spot, which she set in front of me on the way to the door. "Just drink."

"Why?" I asked, watching her press on the tin latch.

The rooster sauntered in, his red-crested head up like a proud king. "Because it keeps you compliant," Lucifer said in his declarative tone.

"With myself, maybe," I rebounded. "But that is because I war with myself—not with God."

"And it begins!" The rooster leapt up, flapping his dark wings to alight upon the counter by the sink. He stared out the window beyond. "I waste myself among repetition."

Deevi, still in her white wife-beater, gray sweatpants, and a pair of clean white Nikes, started toward the fowl. She drew her wings in. "Father, please don't continue our first meeting like this. It is not how I wanted…"

She broke into a daughter's scared, lonely tears.

From my seat I watched in wonder as the rooster lost much of his…cockiness—sorry—and inched toward the weeping half-angel when she leaned against the counter and sobbed.

"You look so much like your mother," Lucifer whispered. His voice cracked. "I've tried. I tried for so long, Deevi."

"But you came for me," she whispered back. "He can't punish you for that. He let you possess Patrick to do it."

"The Lord works in mysterious ways," answered the Morningstar.

The glass of whiskey hovered before my mouth before I downed its contents. The burn in my chest woke me from my stupor. "Well, it's about time we go solve some of those mysteries, Scooby."

"Can you please speak outside references to popular culture?" the rooster asked with a groan. "Be an adult, mortal."

"Father," Deevi chided, wiping at the tears in her eyes.

"Oh, fuck him," I said, reaching into my coat's pocket in the hopes that a joint, or a cigarette, or Advil, had slipped into the folds during my many adventures and had gotten lost. No bloody luck. "And let's get something straight, Lucifer, you're a chicken."

"Am I?" he asked.

My empty glass flew off the table and smashed against the wall behind me, a few of the shards bouncing off the back of my head.

Lucifer stood proud at his deed.

"Oh, spooky," I replied, no worse for wear by this point. "I see that shit every day when I exorcise your mother."

"I don't have a mother," he clucked at me.

"Stop it, both of you!" Deevi said.

This time we both buttoned up, the memory of her power to flatten everything outside still fresh in the mind. Like a shamed little boy, I hung my head with the rooster. We sat in the kitchen for long minutes, waiting for her to speak first. Lucifer eyed me from his place on the counter the entire time.

"Stop staring at him," Deevi told her father. She lifted off the counter's edge, her full weight on her feet. "We need to find Merry and George."

"Why?" Lucifer asked, not breaking his stare. "They are mortals and one's a saint at that. God will not harm them."

"Oh, you're sure about that?" I asked. "They didn't show up handing out tracts and inviting us to breakfast after service. And it's not like God is exactly clear on his definition of harm."

"You act like God thinks at all about you," he said before turning on his claws to face Deevi. "And no, they will not be harmed. If anything, they are probably in a better place than this. I say we leave them to their fates and escape somewhere where I can better protect you."

"And leave them to wonder if we abandoned them?" Deevi asked the fowl, aghast. "They saved me, too."

"No, I saved you," Lucifer said in that parental way. "It was I who told Beherit to reveal the conspiracy to this saint, as it was I who convinced the lwas to reveal your location. By all means, daughter, judge my results! I rescued both him and resurrected the other one when Satan's gambit was revealed, which the saint here witnessed. It was by my hand that you are here, Deevi, and only by my hand can I keep you—"

I exploded. The turmoil of my possession, the endless agony of knowing that not only was I not worthy of God's revelation, but I had been little more than a chess piece, tore too deep. Grabbing the bottle of Green Spot, I launched some glass at him this time, unable to focus on another point to vent my anger.

Deevi caught it before it hit the bird, the aqua vitae splashing on the linoleum floor.

"Keep her?" I screamed at the fowl. "You dirty ancient fucks keep talking about what is yours and what is God's and what isn't, and what is, and..." I had had enough. Years of going from one Italian village to another in the alps, freeing one child from the clutches of Satan and their devil worshiping parents when God wasn't enough, wasn't enough for me anymore. I had walked the entire breadth of Europe, then Africa, then America, and those years flooded back in every day, lost in some hotel room alone, bent over a Bible trying to find one more shred of will to go out there and face down demons.

I had done my duty.

And God hadn't done His to me.

"Father, if you speak one more time then it will be my turn to scream." Deevi crossed the kitchen again, coming to put a hand on my shoulder. "Sit down," she whispered, softly directing me back to the chair at the end of the table. "Just sit down."

I snarled. "But he—Deevi, nobody told me." The tears came, no matter how hard I fought. "Why wouldn't God just tell me? I would have done it if he had. I would have done it."

She guided me back down to my chair, setting the empty whiskey bottle on the wood in front of me. Kissing my temple, she ignored the fussy sounds the rooster made. "We'll rescue Merry and George first," she told me. "And then I'm going to find out why. Do you believe me?"

Drained by emotion, I didn't need to be compelled to tell truth, nor did I need to answer to let her know I did.

2 7

ESCAPE FOR NEW YORK

We left past sunset after Deevi and I packed Merry's old green Yukon, heading for the city on Lucifer's instruction.

"Your mortal friends are not on this plane, or in Time, for that matter," the rooster said as he commandeered the backseat. "What we will need is a nexus, a fixture where the boundaries between dimensions thin. There are enough of these fixtures in New York City to locate a sufficient one."

"You know they just call it New York," I told the rooster from the driver's seat.

Lucifer made no reply.

"Oh, fine," I said, deadpanning him in the rearview mirror.

Deevi sat on the back bench behind the rooster, her glowing wings crowding the cabin. A pair of Merry's air buds in her ears, the light of the smart phone in her hand failed to diminish her golden gaze as we drove in the pitch-black night. The grass hemming in the tire-worn path swished against the truck's sides, a constant beat until we made it to the roads leading back to civilization.

Where did she find those ear buds?

Whatever she watched, it put a smile on her face, so I let her be.

By the time we reached the highway, the quiet had settled too long for my liking. A set of headlights behind me departed the ramp a mile back from where we emerged out of the country, following behind us at an easy pace. Save for a few carrier trucks, that car and the Yukon were the only ones on the road.

"So God gave you permission to possess me, huh?" I whispered.

The fucking rooster didn't even look at me.

"Why?" I asked. "You can at least tell me that."

Lucifer finally deigned to speak. "I don't have to tell you anything beyond what God wishes me to. My daughter was kidnapped, she needed to be found, and he gave me the vehicle to find her—and thought that a devoted saint would be glad that he had been chosen as the Lord's tool."

Leaning back in the gray driver's seat, I spotted a little decal of Papa Legba's veve in the corner of the windshield, the sigil for Vodun's spirit of transition. I hoped the damned fool was right about his brothers and sisters. Angels aren't cuddly, or sweet, or sad, or happy, or possessed of human emotions equal to our scope of perception. The idea of pain in the mortal shell is an unknown concept for God's host.

They feel but not like us.

It made me wonder about Lucifer. "So, what was all that shit back there of deals and custody? It sounded like a spat between divorced parents. If God gave you permission, why are you rebelling?"

"Drive, saint."

If Deevi asked me a question, no matter if I wanted to answer or not, I would have been compelled to. Lucifer spoke with the same power, but instead of answering, I felt my hands squeeze on the wheel in anger. "What? Ruffle your feathers?"

Again, nothing. The miles passed on.

The headlights in my rearview had gotten closer, the bottle cap circles of a large white church van.

"Huh."

"What now?" asked Lucifer.

My turn to be the ass, I didn't reply.

The church van sped up behind us.

The rooster hopped onto the center console I rested my elbow on and faced the rear of the truck. "Saint."

Deevi noticed and took her ear buds out. "What's going on?"

"Nothing," I said, watching the van shift lanes and sidle alongside the Yukon, getting about a meter ahead of me.

Emblazoned on the side of the white painted doors, big pink letters spelled out the name of St. Mary's School for Dignified Ladies —sponsored by New Word Ministries.

"Oh, fuck," I said.

The doors on the van's bay opened. Standing in the back, a pair of teen school girls in button shirts, red skirts, and knee socks raised their AK-47s at us.

"Holy fucking shit," I shouted, wrenching the wheel hard to the left. The Yukon crashed into the van, knocking it off course for a moment and making the girls cut the air with the rat-tat of their rifles. We both swerved, trying to keep steady on the three-lane highway. "Fucking-goddamn-Bible-thumping-cock-sucking—"

Lucifer interrupted. "Steady your course, saint!"

"Fuck you, chicken!"

"Patrick, slow down," Deevi ordered.

The Satanic nun driving the van righted her trajectory on the road and drifted near us again, her child soldiers in the back reset for another volley. I slammed on the brakes, the tires screeching as they thundered by us. One of them tried to pop off a few shots before they fell out of range.

Flaming sword already in her hands, Deevi kicked out the back door of the Yukon.

"Goddammit, we need that," I shouted as the hunk of metal and plastic landed on the asphalt behind us and slid into the darkness.

Lucifer flapped his rich wings, the outside wind moving the feathers on his blue hackle. "Move! Move! Serpentine!"

I slammed my foot on the gas as Deevi dodged out of the SUV, taking to the sky with her sword, casting a molten glow that broke the night's hold on the world. The tires dug into the road as the battered

Yukon skidded to a stop under the stamp of my foot. The school van had reversed gears, hurtling backwards at us. The school girls bunched together in the bay, all five armed with automatic weapons.

"Fuck, fuck, fuck, fuck," I shouted.

Lucifer landed in my lap, his fucking rooster head obscuring my vision. "What now?"

The girls opened fire. Bullets shattered the windshield as the tire on the driver's side popped, dropping the front corner a few inches.

No longer able to keep a straight line if I accelerated, I gripped the wheel hard and nearly bashed the rooster out of the way with my twisting arms in the fight to keep us from slamming into the concrete barriers on either side of the highway. The rim left a rut in the road as we cut hard to the left, but I held us until the brakes broke stopping us. The Yukon slid out to the side, the plastic and steel of the passenger side between us.

More bullets punched holes into the back bench with the plywood splintering as springs in the foam snapped. I fought with the seat belt strapping me in, watching in terror as the school van closed on us.

Deevi came careening out of the sky and rammed the van on its driver's side. The force of the impact knocked the vehicle off its four wheels, sending it rolling into the concrete barrier, the bodies of our young attackers falling out as it dumped them on the curb. The Nephilim took the brunt of her ungraceful landing, her wings curled around so she rolled when she struck the ground.

I got the belt off by the time she got back up, no worse for wear except for the holes the road had torn in her stained clothes. Deevi strode forward as the schoolgirls crawled to their feet with their broken guns in pieces.

I didn't watch what she did to those girls, or the nun, when she reached them with that sword. I chose not to.

That fucking rooster watched everything, though. I think he may have enjoyed it.

28

MCDONALD'S

The van attack, as quick as it began and as quick Deevi had ended it, rattled me enough that I stayed quiet long after, watching the road for more attacks until we found a truck stop outside the city after walking a few hours. Deevi remained sky bound until I jimmied the lock on a carrier van that had seen fair use. With little smell and enough room that she'd fit her wings in the back, I was blessed a second time to discover it was still one of those old models one could flick two wires together, and the engine purred.

Lucifer cleared his throat, standing on the cement by my feet while I hot-wired our new ride. "Morning will be here soon."

I tried hard not to look at him while I climbed into the driver's seat, loosed the parking brake, and put the van in reverse. I backed out of the space with the lights off so whomever was inside getting their coffee or taking a shit wouldn't notice. The sight of it seemed ridiculous enough, if not for the haughty sneer the bastard-rooster somehow made with his tiny beak.

Part of me yearned for George in that moment, as crazy as it sounded.

"Saint, I am speaking to you," the bird said after I allowed him to fly in through the driver's side window and take his place to my right.

I put the van in drive, eyes already on the exit of the gas station parking lot. "Will you hold on?"

The tank full, I turned us back onto the highway.

"Will you speak now?" the rooster asked in the quiet before dawn.

"What now?" I asked, settled in the seat. I was hungry and the signs along our route emblazoned diners, hotels, and more gas stations, until finally the insignia of those golden arches smiled at this weary traveler.

Only two miles.

"We must be careful as we approach the city," Lucifer said. "If we can be so easily attacked by mortal forces in the country it is sensible to surmise that Manhattan will be even more dangerous."

I looked at him. Yes, all angels are this obvious, even Gabriel, but they at least had a sense of humor about it. "No shit?"

"I am not defecating in any way, Saint Patrick," the bird answered, starting at me intently. "The legions of Perdition teem in New York."

"Well, yeah," I replied, focused on the oncoming mile marker. One more mile to a delicious fried hash brown. And coffee. I'd get something for Deevi, but I had no idea what. "That's what makes it so much fun." Lucifer did not laugh at my joke. Fuck him. "Where are we going to find one of these nexuses to find George and Merry?"

The rooster had turned and faced forward in the car seat, perfectly still as always.

Lucifer did not answer my question.

I reached over and snatched him by the neck, yanking him off his shitty little feet.

He squawked, wheezing as those shitty little claws ran in place, unable to control themselves. "Put me down before you regret it!"

Driving with my knee, I smooshed Lucifer into the old, musty passenger seat, his beak buried in the brown cloth as I held him there, pushing his entire body into it. Squeezing my hand around his neck, I almost wished it had snapped in that moment. Wrenching him up, I held the fallen chosen of God and let him curse, breathe, whatever he needed, before depositing him back on the seat.

"You might have murdered this form," he cawed, huffing as he gathered himself.

I saw the sign for my exit and used my left hand to flip the turn signal. "You and I need to get on the same page, bird."

Puffed out and ruffled, Lucifer stood, legs spread.

Preening. This angel was preening at me. Hard.

"God screwed me with you. God screwed you with her," I said, pounding the roof of the van as we crested the top of the ramp. McDonald's lay just to the right, bright like the manger on the night the babe was born. The soft, melted crystals of maple syrup, dolloped in the pancake bun, would elevate the hickory bacon so well...and the softness of the fresh egg? I kept focus on breakfast instead of the rage I felt. "You and I need to work together to get my friends back. To find answers."

"Why would I be in need of finding answers? I have what I want," Lucifer replied.

"And yet you're still a rooster in a world where she's going to be what she is."

He clapped up at that.

I went in. "Won't it be charming when the Christians attempt the obliteration of the demon-chicken? I can see the rags now in the newsstand..."

"I am the Morningstar," he said, but in a defeated tone when he realized the implications I had made. "I'm the brightest light..."

"Sure you are. That's the problem." A right into McDonald's and I zipped into the empty drive-thru.

"Welcome to McDonald's, ready when you are," crackled the voice from the speaker.

"Yeah, I'll have a number five with an extra hash brown and a large hot coffee, and..." I glanced at the Morningstar, who was in the middle of molting over the prospect of never having an inch of his type of normalcy. "What do you think Deevi wants?"

The question caught him. "I..." The rooster's beak hung open, lacking any knowledge. The little thing's heart might have broken in his breast.

It felt good. "Can I get two Egg McMuffins, one large, iced coffee with a pump of chocolate, and another hash brown," I continued, shouting at the speaker.

"Pull around to the window," the tired voice on the other side asked after they gave me the total.

"How do you know she'll like that?" Lucifer asked, solemn.

"I don't." I fished my coat pocket for George's wallet. "But I know more about her than you do, and I know her well enough to know that she isn't going to just walk off with you. She has more sense of responsibility. You're stuck with us until we rescue George and Merry, so you better learn to get along, my feathered..." I shook my head. "Can't call you that, can I?"

Lucifer mulled it over while I paid. The bored lady on the other side of the window handed me that white bag of treasure and we parted ways, me much happier than before and her corporate overlords a few dollars richer.

I pulled off a few miles down the road, put the driver's seat back, and texted "clear."

"Why are you helping now?" Lucifer asked while I sipped hot, black death in a cup. "God has used you for the needed purpose."

"Maybe I want to know that purpose. Maybe I'm tired of being fucked with."

"You're not the first, saint, nor are you special."

Another sip of coffee dimmed my urge to punch him right in the fucking beak. "Doesn't change the fact that I still want to ask those questions."

"God rarely answers."

Off to the east, the sun set the horizon aflame, the fresh light hinting at the most brilliant color of blue. I spotted her in the distance, gliding low to the ground across a field of swaying grass. Her wings cast light on the seeded ends.

"Then I guess he's going to have to make some exceptions," I said. "For all of us."

NOTORIOUS

CHICKEN CHASER

I had collected enough cars over the last week to take at least five families to Disney, but once again we dumped the van in some lot in Jersey City, another one of those boroughs where people moved in hopes of affording their lifestyles, only to stare down the same barrel of the real estate gun always on the prowl. I hot-wired a full-size SUV someone had left in an alley old enough not to have a GPS on it.

I wasn't in the best of moods.

Parked behind a set of empty new builds by the water, Lucifer and I had barely spoken after our little chat. Deevi sat in the back, playing whatever she played on the phone Merry had given her. She tapped her thumbs against the screen, holding it sideways like she had been playing video games all her life.

I looked at her wide, glowing-gold wings in the rearview, fucking realizing that I probably should have kept the carrier van. Out here in Jersey City, overrun with these hipsters, the chance of finding the next car without a digital security system seemed scarce.

"I can't put you on a train," I told her after we ditched the SUV later. We sat on a bench in a small park which overlooked Manhattan's southern districts where progress coupled with easy greed. "Deevi. Deevi!"

"I almost…" She put the phone away from her face, clearly disappointed in something. "Why is the princess always in another castle?"

"Because if she was in the first castle it would be a terribly short game," said Lucifer, perched on her shoulder. "There's just another castle. You can do this."

"Hey," I snapped. "Hey!"

"Sorry," Deevi said, putting the phone in her pocket. The fucking rooster sighed on her shoulder.

"We need to split up," I said, trying to keep everyone on track. How George and Merry dealt with me, I had no idea. "I can't take you on a train to Manhattan with those wings, even if I find a big coat, and the model act will only get us so far now that Dennison Tower got blown up. You need to fly somewhere ahead of us, and we need to find a meeting place. I think Central Park will be safe after dark, for what that is."

"We shall meet you there," said Lucifer. "Deevi, tuck me under your arm."

"Oh, wait a second," I said, a hand out to stop them both. I pointed at the rooster. "You're coming with me in a bag."

"I am not riding in a bag," the rooster replied. "Not for a moment."

"Father, I can't fly high and expect your shell to stay warm enough," said Deevi. "Where is this Central Park?"

"I'm. Not. Getting. In. A. Bag," Lucifer repeated, flapping off his daughter's shoulder and onto the pavement between us. He pecked his way towards my shins, the barbs on his feet bared to flog me.

Deevi caught him by his tail-side like a natural chicken chaser. "No, you don't!"

"Don't speak to me like I'm some impertinent child," he cried, kicking his shitty little legs. "I am your father!"

"And what am I going to do with a talking rooster that proclaims himself Lucifer in public? This is New York," I said, bent over the little bloody bastard. "You would get stomped by foot traffic and I don't give a damn how powerful you are, Foghorn, someone will call animal control. And I can't wait to hear what you'd say to NYPD if they got a hold of you."

"Please, father." Deevi smiled at me, amused. "What if we let you choose the bag?"

The rooster thought on it. "I want to choose the bag."

"This will be so much fun," I said in full sarcasm. "Let's go find one."

Lucifer glared at me for a moment. "It must be a nice bag. With plenty of room."

"Whatever." I pulled out my phone and motioned to Deevi for hers. Opening the compass app on her phone, I turned it back over to her. "Just head north toward the city. Try to stay out of sight, but head for the big, rectangular park in the middle of the island. You'll see a big reservoir right in the center of it."

"And that is Central Park?" she asked, looking northward toward Manhattan.

"Yes, and if you get lost along the way, find somewhere safe on land and call me. Sprint should cover the eastern seaboard, at least," I replied.

"Alright, Saint Patrick." She gave me that glowing smile, and if this actual cockblock next to us hadn't been here, I would've drawn her in for a kiss.

Instead, she did it, reaching forward and taking my hand to pull me in. Our lips met for a brief moment, long enough that the rooster clucked and bothered about our feet, letting his disappointment be known.

"Be careful," I whispered when I stepped back, almost kicking the bird square in the head with my heel.

I swore she laughed as she took to the sky, flapping her wings so hard she ascended in a blink. Praying that none of these damned hipsters were quick enough to snap a pic and post it all over Instagram, I watched her until she disappeared, the glow of her wings vanishing points of light in the sky.

"I'm not happy about this situation," said Lucifer, watching along with me. "But if we must. Come, saint."

The rooster started pecking his way out the alley.

"Hey," I called after Lucifer. "Where do you think you're going?"

"Where we are both going, simpleton." I could literally hear the archangel inside the fowl wanting to desperately whine at his predicament. "To find my carriage."

I sighed, plodding along. I wondered if this is what Daniel felt after taking out that stupid thorn?

30

COCK-A-DOODLE-DOO

etween waking up half naked after the explosion at Dennison Tower, having Lucifer exorcised from my soul, and walking the streets of Jersey City, I hadn't thought up until that point to look in a mirror. A plate glass window beside the sidewalk skipped the thinking part and provided a reflection in the daylight.

My peacoat hung together on its last threads, my jeans were splatted in dirt and chicken shit, and my Doc Martins were beyond filthy and not fashion filthy. I didn't even have a shirt on, leaving the green and gray tats across my chest and stomach exposed. Dressed like Machine Gun Kelly after a plane crashed into him, stepping onto the daylit streets stung my tired, tired eyes. Searching up and down the block, I spotted a row of shops nearby and padded toward them.

Lucifer pranced alongside me, his cape feathers glossy. "Now, for a carrier I will need these specifications if I am to be comfortable—"

"Shut up."

"Excuse me?"

"Shut the fuck up," I repeated with emphasis, placing my foot in front of him to stop his gait. "You can't talk if we're going to do this. Nobody can know that you're Lucifer, or an archangel, or a fucking talking chicken for the matter. Just keep up with me and stay quiet."

159

"I am the Morningstar," he began, to which I rolled my eyes.

"You're my therapy-pet, or whatever those assholes call them. Oh, service animals." I trudged on, beyond giving a fuck. "You're my service chicken. And I'm buying the bag, you little twerp, so move."

The first store to my right offered a fair discount on some brands I wouldn't feel embarrassed stepping out in, and fishing through the pockets of my pants, I found George's black card thankfully had survived the journey with me.

"Okay," I told the rooster. "Stay cool and follow me."

I pushed in the glass door to the department store, allowing Lucifer room to cluck past me like he was any other visitor.

"Excuse me, sir," the girl behind the counter asked. "Is that a rooster?"

My best brogue came out. "Oh, aye," I said, my hand out to display my fowl follower. "This is Jerry. He's my support chicken."

Lucifer puffed up like a balloon, the struggle not to say something warring inside the little fucking pecker. God, I hated this fucking bird.

The lady behind the counter, her hair pulled up in a bun and in designer jeans, side-eyed my obvious lack of cleanliness and gave the bird one more look. "You have money?"

I pulled out my Vatican card. "As much as you'd like to stop asking questions about the chicken."

She knew the proper color of plastic. Coming out from behind the counter, she gave me a dire expression. "Is Jerry trained? Because I don't know how to clean bird shit out of the carpet."

"He'll keep it in." I nudged Lucifer in the fluff to keep him going. "And what's your name, lass?"

"Sheila." The girl kept her eyes on the bird as he pranced before her on the way to the bags. "Are you two going to be long? I have a break in ten minutes and I'm not sure my manager is going to be happy with a rooster in her store when she comes in."

My best smile did nothing to diminish her lack of fucks. "Jerry and me will be quick, Sheila."

I sauntered over to where Lucifer clearly took his time, in front of the only other human in the room, to individually inspect the collection of Louis Vuitton's in the corner. A swank bucket bag trimmed in black leather sat right on the corner of the lowest shelf. He pecked around it appraisingly.

"Too expensive," I said.

That damn rooster glanced back at me like I had interrupted something important.

"Oh, fucking fine." Grabbing the bag, I wandered to the men's section of the store, happy to be away from the bastard.

Out came the smartphone. Thankfully, Deevi hadn't sent me any messages. I worried about her for a second before tapping my thumb on the web app and hitting the big red CNN icon in my favorites.

REV. THOMAS CROMWELL MADE HEAD OF INTERFAITH COUNCIL BY SENATE REPUBLICANS AFTER TERRORIST ATTACK IN NYC.

I stared at the headline for a moment, thinking that finally I snapped again, and so had the world.

Was this it, God?

Was I supposed to just keep marching and marching, marching and marching, until the world jumped off the cliff? What was I to do about your fallen archangel, who violated me? Or his daughter, who made things more and more complicated with every breath I took around her?

What should I have done, God?

Turning to find Lucifer, my ire rose.

Sheila and a few other patrons had congregated around the bloody prideful shit, one of them bent over to stroke the back of his long neck. Not clawing or pecking, he tilted his comb toward this person, eyes shut while making cooing noises that elicited more happy squeals.

"Look at him," said the petter, or Basic White Girl. "He's so nice and soft!"

The little bastard played it up, shaking his curved tail feathers and positioning himself so even more gentle hands could lay on him.

No, I wasn't going to make the jokes. Not for me and not for him.

Fuck that little shitty bird.

"Hey, Jerry," I called.

Lucifer turned his beak my way, and I motioned for him to come over. Rising from his settled position, he hopped down from the bag display and trotted over to me by the men's jeans.

"What are you doing?" I asked.

He looked up at me, saying nothing beyond whatever cocky expression that cock could muster. Smart little shit.

I turned my phone's screen toward him.

If a rooster's beak could drop, Lucifer's did.

Clucking, he tried hard not to speak, a moment of angst I surprisingly took little joy in. His little beady eyes flicked up at me, and he headed back to where the girls still waited, watching and whispering to themselves about what the cute little bird would do next. He plopped down at their feet, and in adoration Basic White Girl fell to her knees, back to stroking his cape. Lucifer did not cluck or move, staring at the nearby blue carpet with a deep sense of dread on his face.

He knew something.

Wow She Is Too Beautiful Latina knelt beside Basic White Girl and joined in, with only Sheila keeping a healthy eye of distrust toward the bird.

I found a black cable-knit sweater for me, a few pairs of jeans for me and Deevi, some backless, long-sleeved shirts I hoped she would like, and kept my boots. The dirty old bastards deserved the chance at a few more miles, and there were definitely a few more miles to go.

31

FLYNN AND ELLIS

Lucifer rode next to me on the One's hard green bench from South Ferry, his bright red comb and wattle sticking out of the Louis Vuitton bucket bag that cost the Church five hundred dollars, but I thought would go well with the things I got for Deevi.

I had plans to make her carry that fucking shitbird.

"You're glaring at me again," Lucifer said.

Shitbird.

I raised my head and searched the train. Like the shepherds, only three others inhabited the carriage with me, all women.

The first was a wee one, maybe in her late teens at the end of the car on my side, bundled up in a trench coat two sizes two big and with big-rimmed readers that made her seem bookish if not for the high-gloss French manicure on her fingers and the recently trimmed ends of her in-season bob-whatever. There would be ten more of her at the next stop.

Across and down the way, the second girl had her earbuds in, listening to something about Satan and tequila by the way her torn fishnets lanced up her toned legs, like some acid-punk Lady Gaga. Big, colorful tattoos raced across her shoulders, down the outside of her thighs, and the long designs on the shins spoke of someone who clearly did not have a large issue with pain. She also tried to hide a switchblade in her cut-off goth jacket but sucked at it. Probably wasn't even trying in the first place. This city.

The third, at the other end of the cart and also on the other side, was a pretty woman in a white dress blouse and black skirt, her heels crossed in a position that did not seem to take any pressure off. Her white earbuds in as well, she watched something flash across her phone screen with maniacal focus.

None of them paid a lick of attention to us.

I went back to staring at the window in front of me, watching my reflection bubble and bend over the struts in the tunnel.

"I said you were glaring at me," the rooster repeated.

"You can't talk."

"I am the Morningstar," he said.

I fucking freaked out, though as quietly as I possibly could. "Do you know how damn weird that sounds? Do you understand that when you say that nobody but me knows what that means? Not everyone is walking around all day caring about God, or you, or the Devil, or anything at all having to do with you miscreants, and if they did, they would tear the lot of you down. So please, shut up."

If a rooster could lean away, Lucifer did, his neck feathers ruffled.

The subway car skidded to a stop at Rector Street. The first girl, the wee one in the oversized trench coat, scuttled out of the cart.

"She's going to go drink with some young stockbrokers before midnight so she can make it through old, lecherous men who can actually afford the taste of her flesh," Lucifer said. "She will take the money and pay for her tuition at NYU and still graduate with enough debt that remaining a prostitute will seem a better option than the mind-numbing toil of a corporation, where she would only continue to sleep around anyway."

"What?" I asked, my attention drawn back to him.

The train got moving again.

"I understand that this is not perfect, Saint Patrick," Lucifer began, "but I can also understand why you feel the way you feel."

"Don't fucking try to apologize, Jerry," I said. "You don't know shit."

The rooster raised his beak at me, lacking his usual majestic bearing. "You think you're the only one that God presented his 'mysteries' to?"

The train made it to Chambers, a stop I remembered only because Merry had taken me somewhere around there for Moroccan food. The thought of her drew my thoughts away from my own troubles. The words of the Iwas haunted me, whispering about how we would never be together again, at least not in love.

Was that only what they had meant?

The lady in the blouse and skirt got up, pulling her buds from her ears as she marched out onto the world, a defiant expression on her face against whatever came at her.

"She murdered her husband and his much younger lover, their secretary, and is going to the boardroom right now to lay majority shareholder status at the feet of all the men she's going to fire." Lucifer sighed, his feathers smooth again. "The police will be there to arrest her after the maid's daughter discovered the bodies in their Chelsea apartment fifteen minutes ago. The little girl was supposed to be at school, but her mother could no longer afford it because the murderer refused to pay her full wages. She will spend the rest of her days in prison, but she will never understand what she did wrong. Some will even celebrate her for it and make a movie."

"What's your point?"

"God gives permission to all things in his dominion, whether or not everyone hears it, or if it is of good or evil. I was given permission by God directly to inhabit you and lead you along the path to find Deevi. God allowed that and I took advantage of it to save my daughter."

"It doesn't excuse it. I've given much to the Lord."

"And flaunted your vices before him as well."

Fucking goddamn chicken.

At that moment Acid Punk Gaga pulled her buds out of her ears. "Okay, you know what, this is fucking too much." Getting up on her spiked, three-inch heeled boots, she sauntered over, all tattooed curves and torn-cotton glories. She plopped down on the bench across from me and the rooster and leaned forward, cleavage and three different colors of eye-liners staring right at me. "And I sing, bitch, so don't even try to fool me that you're some ventriloquist. I heard everything fucking thing that cock said."

I cringed a bit when she used the word. "Okay, love, you got me. I have a talking rooster."

"What's his name?" she asked.

I sighed. "Lucifer."

"Like the devil?"

"I'm not the devil," Lucifer said. "It is an erroneous misconception created by the Catholic church and the Protestant denominations, starting with the frightfully inept medievalists, who are too lazy to read and didn't want to deal with distinguishing me from basic star systems, let alone the Devil. Who I am not."

"So you do speak." Acid Punk Gaga glanced his way, joyfully amazed. "So what are you guys up to?"

"Just riding the train," I said. "Trying to get my friend here back to the park."

"Oh, Central Park, huh?" She met eyes with me.

Oh, no. Those eyes.

"Yeah, where you headin'?" I asked, keeping things neutral.

"The park." Her black-painted lips parted to reveal those pretty white teeth in a suggestive smile. "Say, can I touch your cock?"

I gave her a sympathy chuckle. "I'm sure Lucifer will let you pet him if you ask."

She laughed with me. "Not the rooster, handsome."

"I commend you for the convenient location of the park, madame." Lucifer then spoke right to me, as if she no longer existed. "She is planning to take you to the park, have intercourse with you, and while doing so kill you at the moment of mutual ejaculation by slitting your throat with the knife in her...is that really a jacket? She is also a lawyer for a non-profit."

Acid Gaga balked at the rooster, at a sudden loss of her bravado. "How do you know all that?"

"Crack her one?" I asked him.

The rooster sighed again. "This case seems appropriate."

"Just go on, miss," I said to Acid Gaga, nodding her away. "God will get you. Trust me."

Her hand went to the inside of her frayed jacket instead, failing to reach the switchblade before I tagged her dead in the jaw. We left her there at the next stop and walked the rest of the way after that. The bag made it easy to keep the rooster quiet.

32

STRAWBERRY FIELDS

The rooster and I sat in the park near Strawberry Fields until the sun set behind the hills. I tapped Deevi's number and put the phone to my ear.

She picked up after it rang twice. "I'm by the lake."

"Which one?" I asked. "The reservoir or the little one?"

"Which one is which?" she whispered. I heard a rush of air at the other end of the phone, and not far to my east a beautiful woman ascended to the bronzing skies with glowing wings.

"Oh, nothing to fucking worry about there," I said to no one in particular. Even at sunset, the city was packed with people, and the park no less.

"I see her," said Lucifer, and he threw his head back and crowed.

I dropped the bag I carried him in, startled by the sudden noise.

"Be careful," he said, wriggling from the black leather bucket. He shook out his feathers before tossing his head back for another screeching note.

"Oh, I hear you," Deevi said, and the call ended on her side, which was just as well considering how quickly I was moving to shoo Lucifer further down the sidewalk, away from where a crowd might gather for an angel and her talking rooster.

"Get on, you daft bird," I ordered, kicking him in the tail feathers before I grabbed his bag. We marched deeper in, past the popular spots and to a fenced off area behind the Swedish Cabin or whatever it was called.

Deevi came around the corner, her wings drawn close to her back and with that big, happy smile on her face.

I tried to match it. "Did anyone see you?"

"Just some children earlier in the day, but I talked to them and they promised not to tell anyone," she said, taking the bag of clothes when I handed it to her. She looked me up and down, with my new cable-knit sweater and fancy jeans. "You look nice."

"Thank you," I said, and with that alone, the tension broke. I loosened for a moment, standing without a care.

Lucifer walked in between us. "Turn around, Saint Patrick, and let my daughter have the dignity of her nudity."

"You act like I haven't seen it before," I quipped.

"He has," added Deevi, much to her rooster-daddy's ire.

"Well, I'm here now and—"

Deevi pulled off her tattered wife-beater, exposing her pair of glories—

The rooster crowed at us. "Turn around, Saint Patrick!"

"Fuck off, chicken." I paid him no mind from that moment. "I got you some shirts," I told Deevi, lowering my gaze. "We can go get you some better underwear and shoes, later."

"Why would I need underwear?" she asked.

"Because you need to be decent," Lucifer said. "Why are neither of you looking at me?"

Fitted with her new clothes, she could have been any of the would-be goddesses marching around NYC, off to work their job at the shops in hopes that the right agent or the right person in the right place would walk in and sweep them into a life of money and fame. Rarely worked that way these days. Only the wings hampered it all, which we couldn't fix in the moment.

Sticking her old, ratty clothes in the shopping bag, she took my hand when I offered it. The warmth of her skin calmed me further, and for the first time I didn't allow the overwhelming creep of the world to fall upon me. We squeezed our hands a few times before we broke contact.

The rooster made an unhappy sound when he saw that.

"Ready to go?" I asked.

Deevi glanced around the park. "What will we say about my wings?"

I wiped my hands down my tired face. The grim reality of it all set in, and I decided that was the time to define it even more. "Cromwell is alive."

Her golden eyes widened.

"It's okay," I said. "I don't think he knows we're here in the city. Not yet."

"You assume that Satan would only possess one form," Lucifer said in his pithy, rooster voice. "He could be in many cities."

"So what would you do, bird?" I asked, not breaking my shared eye contact with Deevi.

"You will have to take to the sky again, Deevi," Lucifer instructed. "Patrick has found an adequate bag—"

"Which was $500," I added.

"And we must go and locate your friends. There is a nexus somewhere on this island. If we can find this split in time and space, we can attempt a rescue."

"All right," said Deevi, refocused. "I actually enjoy the time above, believe it or not. I didn't get to fly as much in Syria."

"I can call you when we get to a hotel or whatever we find—one with a balcony or roof access, hopefully. Just keep your phone," I said.

"Okay." Deevi leaned over and kissed me sweetly on the mouth. "I'll go."

She took the skies again in two great flaps, defying gravity in a way humanity only dreamed. She flew into the starry night, the light pollution from the street lamps covering her ascent.

I looked down at the rooster stewing beside his black leather chariot.

"What?" I asked. "I can't help it if she does it."

Lucifer flattened his feathers. "It is not your fault. She takes after me."

"The forwardness?"

He clucked. "The rebellion."

"So where to?" I asked, resigned to my continued journey. I preferred George for company—he'd at least be good in a fight.

"You run in circles of heathens," Lucifer said as he hopped into the zippered opening. He dug himself down and roosted, his bright head and glossy tail poking out like before. "Wouldn't one of them know where to find a nexus?"

"You greatly overestimate the powers of these New Agers. Lot of talk and socializing, less evoking and summoning."

He clucked again.

An idea hit me. "Why didn't I think of that?"

"What?"

"Brooklyn."

BREAKING AND ENTERING

I had Deevi smash the window by Merry's front door in the middle of the night, allowing me to sneak my arm through the jagged hole to let us in. We turned on the lights and I found enough black trash bags and masking tape to make it look like the owner had gotten themselves locked out and had to force their way in, leaving us safe in the empty brownstone of the missing Vodun priestess.

Lucifer sensed it the moment he walked through the doorway. "There is a nexus here."

"Right-o, chicken," I said, stepping back to review my handiwork with the window. "It'll be upstairs on the second floor, across the hall from Merry's bedroom."

The damn bird got on his way up the steps, hopping each one while muttering something about me and the height of doors.

Kicking off her Nikes, Deevi went to the kitchen, leaving smudges on the tile with her dirty feet. She opened one of the windowed cabinets and got herself a clean glass. Turning on the faucet, she sipped the 'champagne' of tap waters, or whatever bullshit this fucking city wanted the world to believe that week.

"Hey, sit down," I told her, pulling out a chair at the table in the breakfast nook.

Leaving her glass behind, Deevi came and sat down, her wings crowding the area in front of the bay window. Thankfully, Merry always kept the shades pulled shut, with the slaughtering chickens and conjuring spirits and all that.

"Hungry?" I asked, pulling up the Seamless app on my phone after I logged into Merry's Wi-Fi.

"Anything will be fine," she said with a weary smile. "I flew all day."

"I know." I passed the phone into her hands. "Have whatever you like."

She nearly grabbed the smart phone and started searching Brooklyn's wide range of offerings, leaving me a moment to go to the sink myself. Pulling out a small plastic tub I had watched Merry use to wash her ritual tools so many times before, I squirted some soap into it. It filled with suds while I retrieved a clean hand towel from the drawer beside the gas range.

Lifting my basin, I walked it over to where she sat and put it in front of her.

Squatting down, I pulled one of her dirt-stained feet close with my left hand while plunging the dry washcloth into the warm tub. Rubbing the grime from the top of her right foot, I scrubbed until I found her in-step.

"What are you doing?"

She had put down the phone, looking dead at me.

"Washing your feet," I said. "Find something to eat and let me get this done." I balled the rag in my hand and wiped the bottom of her foot.

She bit her lip and playfully kicked me in the face with the other, finally breaking out in gentle laughter.

"Stop," I said, grabbing her other foot.

"Why are you so sweet to me, Patrick?"

"I want to be," I said, compelled by her speech.

"But you don't have to wash my feet," she said. "Nobody has to do that for me."

"Would you like me to stop?" I asked, the exhaustion of the last few days hammering home. My eyelids were weighed with sandbags. Stress invaded my shoulders and neck in a dull, constant ache.

"No," she said, shaking her head.

Her expression changed.

Those golden eyes would not let me go.

She dove forward, pushing me onto my back against the floor. Her mouth pressed to mine, a soft tongue sneaking past my lips before I could take a breath. Her arms wrapped around my head and neck. My feeble attempt to push her off ended when she threw one of her wings over and rolled me atop of her.

I pushed up and away. "He's upstairs," I whispered, gasping.

She pulled me back down, her hot breath on my ear. "I know."

Deevi nibbled the bottom of my earlobe, like she knew somehow that it would get to me, before licking the opening of the canal.

That did it.

I shuddered, barely able to keep in a moan as she expertly undid my belt buckle, not fumbling as she had the first time. Her hand slipped in my jeans, spurring me to action.

"Wait," I said while she yanked off my sweater, which I let her do out of fear that she'd tear the damn thing. Like I was some sort of sex jungle-gym, she pulled herself up on me, using my shoulder and the back of my neck as handholds before planting another deep, needing kiss.

Somewhere in the tussle to get free she held me against the kitchen's stainless-steel fridge, the chill setting my nerves alight. She yanked down my jeans and I bobbed out in front of her. She dropped her own pants in a rehearsed move. Deevi stroked me.

"We can't," I uttered, without the strength to fight temptation.

"Why not?" she asked, hungry.

I blurted it out. "I can't get you pregnant."

"Then pull out."

I looked at her like she had said something obscene, which drew from her a wicked smile. She came close again, biting at my neck. "I'm

Lucifer's daughter, after all," she said to me in that husky, please-fuck-me voice. "Don't you want to get back at that shitty rooster?"

I started ripping the dials off the gas range.

She pulled off her shirt, standing there and grinning before I pulled her in and sat her naked ass on top of the stove. Searching for the correct angle, razor-sharp feathers kept appearing near my face.

We abandoned the kitchen and found the widest piece of wall on the first floor, the next room across the eave. She wrapped us together in her wings while we put cracks in the dry wall.

34

THEM APPLES

I washed the front of my pants three times in the sink before drying them in the oven. They stunk of sex in a way I had never smelled sex stink. Wordless after our long-awaited misdeed, we spent the time making out and laughing at nothing, knowing we had left Lucifer upstairs for more than an hour and had not been the quietest about the fact.

He sat in the middle of Merry's ritual room when we walked in, his displeasure as clear as it could be on his rooster-face.

"Are you refreshed?" he asked Deevi, unable to look at my shit-eating grin.

I tried, but I couldn't keep my peace. "You and God had it coming, you stupid, stupid bird. I didn't teach her about pulling out."

"Well, I certainly didn't," the rooster shrieked at me, popping up to his shitty little legs. Back in my boots, I knew I could kick him to at least the midfield if I tried.

"Have you found a nexus?" Deevi asked her irate father, displaying a pleasantness that probably took the heat off me.

"It is here in this wall." Lucifer pecked his way to the Wall of the Lwas, where Merry had helped me contact the Vodun spirits on the quest to find Deevi. A weird sense of guilt rose in me.

I had banged my new and probably permanent lover in my last lover's house.

I probably wouldn't tell Merry about it. "What do we need to open it? I know where we can get some juju."

"We will not require chemical assistance to access the place between," Lucifer said with some disdain. "We merely need to sacrifice a goat and smear the blood on the wall in the proper design, and I shall speak the incantations. From there we will—"

"Where the fuck am I supposed to get a goat at this hour?" I asked, interrupting.

The rooster sighed at me like I was stupid. "From a farm. I imagine that is where they keep goats."

I should have kicked for a goal, aiming him at one of the blacked-out windows. "We just came from a farm. And there aren't any goat farms in this city."

"Is there an alternative to not slaughtering an animal in our friend's home?" Deevi asked.

"We could make a facsimile, but it would take time to gather the proper ingredients," the rooster replied.

"Why do you need a bloody goat in the first place?" I asked, feeling some unwanted errands coming on.

"I need the fat, meat, and blood of a goat, though a living goat would be better as the reagents would be fresh, for the Lord God is fickle about his meats," said Lucifer. "But we could do it with oil, vegetables, and fresh apples alone, if need be."

"What a long and mighty quest to undertake," I said with deep, intended sarcasm. Apparently he hadn't paid a lick of attention to what a grocery store was in his visits with me. "Stay here and do whatever it is you do." A better thought caught me. "Just stay here."

Deevi followed me out. "Where are you going, Patrick?"

"There's a bodega down the street that will open in a few hours. I was hoping to get some sleep."

"Where are you going to do that?"

I nodded for her to follow me to Merry's room across the hallway, where her funky California King awaited. The blankets still askew from when she had left, I climbed across the mattress and plopped down in one of the corners. Not a couch, not a floor, or a subway bench, the ache of my battered and tired body sank into the old thing, the smells of the past welcoming me home.

Deevi crawled atop of me, resting her head on my chest. Her wings fell over us like a wave of shining feathers that somehow leveled themselves to the exact light needed for me to fall asleep.

"How long do you think we have?" she asked, her words vibrating in my ribcage.

I checked my phone, fishing it out of my jeans and setting an alarm for morning before I tossed it on a nightstand. The thought of a new burner came and went like the brush of a breeze. "I'm not leaving 'til seven."

"And what time is it?"

"Three. We have four hours."

She enclosed her left wing over us, the light gentle and warm. Deevi laid her hand on the mound of my groin, squeezing gently. "Plenty of time."

"That'll kill me," I said, pulling her hand off my aching self. "Next time you need to be the one who takes."

"I might like that."

I glanced down my nose at her. She looked up at me with that little smirk, her wandering hand on my stomach. God knows why I loved her so much, but I did. No matter the urge, or the pull, I loved her with parts of me I didn't think existed.

Not even for God.

But like God, did she come by it honestly?

I combed my fingers through his soft brown hair. "I'm scared."

"Why?" Those gold eyes trapped me. "Why are you scared, Patrick?"

"I'm just a man, at the end of all of this. Like Job." The weight of the thought struck me harder than I planned, putting a lump in my throat. Maybe I had wanted her to pull the truth out of me, and now I didn't like it. "I'm just me."

She nuzzled my throat and kissed it. "You're mine, too."

I took it as well as I could, summoning a smile.

She scooted up, resting her body across mine. Stroking my temple, she studied my face.

"What?" I whispered.

Deevi sighed, her perfect brow furrowed in thought. "Are you still going to take me to Dublin?"

"The moment I find a way," I said. "By boat or air, I'll do it."

"Well, I better hope for a boat." She tapped me on the nose with her finger. "I don't think I can fly you across an ocean."

We laughed, and joked, and sighed, and then somewhere in there slept for a few hours. At least she did.

35

HOLE IN THE WALL

I came back to the house by mid-morning, carrying plastic shopping bags stuffed with all the things the damn rooster wanted.

I juiced the apples for two hours in search of the needed "blood" while Lucifer directed Deevi to draw the appropriate Enochian symbols, where even my familiarity was eclipsed by a far more fluent tongue and her masterful hand. After a few rounds of practice, she produced the elegant sigils her father thought met the requirements.

The bird sang songs in low, quiet notes for a long time in a language I couldn't comprehend before instructing me to light a semi-circle of white candles around the Wall of the Lwas.

"What will happen when...things happen?" I asked Lucifer once I flicked off my lighter. Always a good question to ask first in the middle of magic, no matter if it was divine, infernal, or supernatural.

"When I open the nexus, I will release myself from this rooster, who may die in the transition," Lucifer said, facing the robin's egg-painted wall. "If he does not, he shall be fine, but he cannot be allowed to escape. I will need to repossess him after I guide your friends out of the nexus as quickly as possible so my brethren do not track me back to this place, though they shall have a rough idea of where we are. The destruction that would ensue would make this mission a moot point."

"So what are we to do?" Deevi asked.

"Wait here," said the rooster. "I am the Morningstar. They are only my siblings."

"Oh, only 'siblings'," I said like it was nothing. "What if you don't make it?"

The shitty little bird glanced my way. "You will need to run."

Searching Merry's ritual chamber, I spotted the old wooden chair from the seventies I had taken many trips on while blasted out of my mind. I dragged it to the center of the room, about five feet from where the rooster stood at the edge of his space. Thankfully I had already shut the door.

"Be sure to get both Merry and George," I said as I plopped down. "Both of them, Lucifer."

"I know what I am sent to do, saint."

Deevi joined her father, kneeling beside him so the rooster could hop atop her lap. No noise came from me as I watched parent and child, divided so long by the unknowable mysteries of God, embrace like it was the last time. She wiped her tears away when she opened her arms again, allowing Lucifer to step back down and assume his place at the central point of his altar.

Rising off her knees, her flaming sword seared into existence, glowing bright red as Deevi held it by the hilt. The illumination cut our shadows onto the floor.

Lucifer crowed, loud and long, rising and falling in more of a yodel. The candles flared, their flames extending like rising spires of needle-fire. He let out one last, mournful crow, and silenced before the bird slumped to the floor.

Nothing happened until the rooster popped back to his feet, frantically awake, and took a giant white shit in the harsh light of Deevi's sword.

"Well, I guess he left," I said, squinting against her weapon's wrathful glow.

"Why can't I see the nexus?" Deevi asked.

I lifted a hand to block out her light. "Maybe you need to be bollocksed on the juju."

"So how will we know when they come back?"

"I haven't a clue, darling." I removed the hand, unable to direct my gaze in a way to avoid the light. "Could you put that out?"

The sword of hellish light zapped from her hands to nothingness, returning the room to the low ambiance of the candles arrayed around the wall. "So…how long?"

Shrugging my shoulders in the chair, I put my knees wide and leaned back, the hard wood digging my spine a bit. "Until we don't have to wait anymore."

Deevi, hands on hips and arms akimbo, grunted. "Damn."

I laughed. I don't know why, it was just funny. "So what do you want to do?"

She had already mastered that conspiring look.

I closed my legs. "Still sore."

She chuckled at that, her wings fluttering. "Twice damned."

When had she become a jokester?

The rooster crowed loudly, balanced on one leg and flapping his wings like a maniac as more white shit squirted from him.

Deevi sauntered over and sat on my right leg, her wings balanced so she could face the bird. "Do you think it is too late to actually go and find a goat?"

"That would be cliched. What about a dog? There's so many damned dogs in this city and he'd blend in perfectly."

Her wings may have brightened at the suggestion. "Like a puppy?"

"What about a sloth?" I asked aloud, honestly wondering where we might steal one. "That would work real, real well."

She shifted on my lap, throwing her arms around my shoulders. "That bird didn't act like a normal bird when my father possessed him. Who knows what a sloth might do?"

"True. I just don't want anything with teeth or claws. And kickable, at least," I said, nodding at the rooster.

Deevi stoppered her laughter, a hand over her mouth. Rocking for a few moments on my lap, she settled. "Well, at least we both know one thing."

"What's that?"

"Your lap isn't bruised." That golden glance came my way, satisfied at her deduction. "Which means you have time."

"Why do you want to have so much sex?" I asked, blunt about it.

Deevi didn't seem bothered by the question, nor in her reply. "Because you are beautiful, Saint Patrick," she declared. "And you are the most precious thing in my world. Why would I not want to mate with you before it's too late?"

Dammit. "We're going to get caught one of these days," I said. "And considering your side of the family, I don't like my chances."

"But how do I compare?" Deevi held my chin and kissed me on the mouth, silencing me before I got out another word. Like the last time in this room, my head swam.

Time froze as she loved me. Her lips on mine, the air seemed to pause. I could hear swords clash. Deevi broke first and looked at the blue Wall of the Lwas, standing straight up. I caught the tail-end of flashes at the corner of my sight.

"Oh, no," I said, not ready. "Is your spit like LSD?"

"I don't know what that is, Patrick." Deevi summoned her sword of fury, its blade bubbling back into reality. "If we run, where are we running?"

I had nothing but my rosary in my pocket. Hands up in panic, I searched the room for a weapon, one of Merry's tools, anything when I noticed our resident fowl.

The rooster trotted over to the edge of the candles, threw his head back, and crowed.

Then George and Merry appeared, invisible one second and simply there the next, popped out of thin air. Dressed in the same clothes they had been wearing when taken, they gaped in shock, heaving hard, heavy breaths.

"You're back," I said, breaking the sudden silence.

Merry turned in my direction. "Tater?"

Standing between the feet of our rescued friends, the rooster crowed, turning on his shitty little feet before dashing toward the door. "Run," Lucifer said in the bird's suddenly masculine tone. "Run for your lives!"

3 6

RUNNING FOR OUR LIVES

here's my fucking sword?" George screamed as we all piled down the stairs to the first floor, Merry between us as she held up a basket of things she had torn out of her closets in the bedroom and shoved into a bright green bin. Half bugout, half weird, I didn't get time to really look at any of it.

"Get a fucking move on!" she shouted.

"Where's my sword?" George said, turning to glare at me as he stepped aside to let her by.

I held my hands out, recalling why I often tired of the man. "Left it behind at the house in Jersey?"

His glare brightened his gray eyes. "You left it behind?"

"Sorry for rescuing you," I said calmly, stepping around him. "Now fuck on, we need to start boosting cars before the archangels arrive." Stifling my terror at the prospect, I shouted up the steps. "Deevi, you coming?"

Backed to the top of the steps, the light of Deevi's sword reddened the golden glow of her wings as she waited for our heavenly pursuers to walk out of the bedroom and start the party. Lucifer backed away with her, stationed at her heels, beak set toward whatever father and daughter waited for.

"Coming! Grab my clothes," she replied in calm pleasantness, still facing the hallway. Her expressive frown did not match the tone.

"Come help," I said, pulling George by his lapel.

He stripped off his vestment and shoved it in a pocket as we thundered down the stairwell. "Oh, fuck," he said, rifling through all his coat's compartments, "did you grab my Bible? Or my rosary?"

"They're in Deevi's bag." I pulled out the Vatican Black and handed it to him over my shoulder. "Had to buy us clothes and food."

"Of course," said George. "That rooster still Lucifer?"

"He is," I said, my bare feet slapping the tile at the bottom.

"Bloody hell."

I went for the sitting room, where I had left my boots. "Figure out how we get to La Guardia."

Merry met us at the kitchen entryway with two baskets, the second heaping full like the first. "Are you two still here? Where's my fucking Yukon?"

"Ditched it in Jersey," I snapped. "Now come on. I need you to do that trick you did back in Port Au Prince."

The thing a lot of people don't know about New Yorkers is that most of them think the city is safe, enough so that plenty of dumb people left their cars unlocked outside the restaurants, bodegas, what had you. Some of them even left their keys in the cup holder.

Never needed them in a pinch when I had Merry.

Running down the block, George called first when he found a large, black Escalade pulled up before the next set of apartment buildings. "We'll fit!"

Meeting him by the vehicle's driver-side door, Merry shoved one of her baskets into George's arms, then pressed her finger to the locking. Uttering a few words to a few spirits, the car popped open.

"Get the back bench down!" I watched the streets as George loaded Merry's basket in the back, threw our things in after, and dodged around to the front of the truck. A posh boy from Birmingham had the black beast purring in a minute. Deevi and Lucifer exited Merry's house, the rooster in the lead while his daughter let her sword pop out to wherever it hid when not in use.

"Pull out, George," I shouted, wedged in the very back by Deevi's sharp wings as she dove into the back bench. Merry loaded into the passenger seat, carrying Lucifer in one arm before she placed him down on the black leather console.

Nobody moved fast enough for me. "We need to get going!"

"They're watching us," the rooster said as George put the Escalade into gear. Lucifer gazed through the windshield, his avian eyes peeled for danger. We turned out into the street.

Merry jabbed George in the arm. "Put some weight on it, English!"

Down the road we rushed, headed east toward Queens, much faster than we should have. The rooster scampered beneath his daughter's seat and marched the floor before he reached my end of our cramped space, hopped up on my bench, and started to search outside the truck.

"What?" I asked Lucifer, noticing how intent he went about it. "What are you doing?"

"They're above us," the rooster said with a note of confusion. "The archangels are circling above us."

"Where?" George called, sinking in his seat to get an angle at the empty sky. "I can't see them!"

Merry started crying.

"Mortals can't see them," said the rooster, transfixed on whatever lay above us outside the truck. "Not unless we want you too."

"I see Uriel." Deevi pointed out the window on the driver side, trying to get her wings to bend in a way so she could turn.

"Where's Michael?" Lucifer asked.

"Stop that," George yelled at her. "I can't see out the back."

"Stop moving, Deevi," I pleaded, putting my hand on the shoulder I could reach without having her feathers rip my arm apart.

She calmed her wings. "Sorry."

"Where's Michael?" Lucifer scurried his way between her and I to get to the rear window.

Brooklyn passed by us, on the sidewalks, in front of the shops. New Yorkers carried on about their day in relative peace, caught in the daily humble and grind of the sleepless city.

There were so many people. Too many.

"Incoming!" Lucifer crowed. "Twelve o'clock, Saint George!"

At the upcoming intersection two cabs crashed into each other head-on, throwing one of the drivers through the windshield in a bloody heap. George veered hard to the right, turning us down a residential side-street before we got near the accident. A parked car, uninhabited by a driver, turned out of its spot on the curb. The front left headlight of the Escalade crunched against its panel. Steel sheared against steel, ripping paint off. Trained by the best, George revved on the gas and barged us through the next two that suddenly swung out as well.

"Careful, you wank," I shouted before his break and skid smacked us into the corner of a small hatchback, knocking the wind from me. Deevi grabbed my limp hand and pulled me across the seats beside her, one strong arm over me to keep me where I lay across her lap like a ragdoll.

"Faster, Saint George!" cried Lucifer.

The patron saint of England reversed gear, pulling the shard of our bumper out of the cheap blue plastic of the hatchback's, and shoved the stick back into first.

"Shut up, you fucking Satanic bird," the knight growled, turning his wheel hard to the left as he mashed the accelerator.

The Escalade skidded into a fishtail, the backend smacking a parked car across the street. Bolting from the curb, George growled a second time when he pushed ahead, racing against his own fear and the unseen foes around us. Head-on to heartache we went, groaning and gasping every time our driver dodged an errant car or a sudden pedestrian shoved into the street by an invisible force.

"Open the back," Deevi said. "I can draw them off."

"No," Lucifer and I said in unison.

"Nobody goes without each other," I added. "Not again!"

Tearing north through Queens, the improbable took on a new strategy, causing more accidents and hazards along the street instead of on it. Places we might have turned for escape ground to a halt by a surprise fender bender, or the lights malfunctioning in the middle of a pedestrian walkway, causing both drivers and pedestrians to teeter on the edge of uncertainty.

"Slow down," I said from the back. "They're just following us. They'll keep…" I lost my breath in the excitement.

George pumped the brakes. We came to a stop at a red light, and sat there, waiting for the inevitable to descend upon us.

Nothing came.

"Do you see them?" I asked whoever answered first.

"I do," said Deevi. "They are still flying above us in a circle."

"Why?" Merry asked, the side of her face pressed against the window to her right so she could search above. "Why are they waiting?"

"Because," said Lucifer. "When we stop at our destination, they will kill you all and retake my daughter once we step outside. We ride to our dooms."

Fucking shitty little bird.

DETAILS

Deevi put her hand on my chest while I stared up at the cloth ceiling of the Escalade, unable to think of anything to do in the moment. We drove towards death.

Tears ran down her cheeks.

I reached up with my far hand and wiped them off the right side of her face. "Where did they take you, George? Merry? Did they take you to Heaven?"

George didn't speak.

"Merry," I called. "Where did you go?"

"They went nowhere," said Lucifer, standing by my feet on the floor. The red ring around his beady eyes seemed brighter than usual. Could roosters weep? "My brethren are of the highest order. If they do not think you deserve to roam the halls of the Platinum Polis, why would they dignify you by bringing you there?"

I pointed down at him. "Shut up. Merry's talking."

"No, I'm not, Tater," the priestess in the front seat said in the weakest voice I had ever heard her use.

Being a priest or priestess for any faith required one to walk among the masses of the sick, the broken, offering to heal mind and body by tending the wounds of the soul. I quit because the Church became too large to assuage my doubts about the work we did, but I'm no Martin Luther. I respected the Chair for what he was trying to do in the world.

But at some point, it isn't enough to try. At some point you had to make good on your words. The way Merry sounded, every single thing she had dealt with in the world, words or otherwise, had been a walk in the park compared to what she went through with Michael and his kin. Hers was the voice of someone who had seen worse than atrocity and now had to live past it.

Whatever my two friends had witnessed, they would never be the same.

I tried to keep my own tears from coming.

Why God? Why punish them? One was doing your work better than I ever have, and the other one is just some damaged soldier you keep hurting.

For your sake, and your sake alone.

Speak nothing to me, fine, but both did the work.

For you. If not this saint, why not ones who deserved it?

"Because God lies," Lucifer said aloud.

"God damn you, father!" Deevi kicked her feet in all directions.

The top of her foot struck Lucifer in the breast. Like a football he bounced off the window, rolled back into the floor, and lolled to the side. He lay there for a moment, and I thought him dead until he sprang up, feathers flared for battle.

"Why, daughter, would you betray me in this moment?" the rooster cried in his angelic, booming voice.

Those beady little eyes glowed gold before they sputtered out when she pinned him against the back of Merry's seat by his long neck.

"He was praying," Deevi said. She set him back on the ground gently. "And you couldn't just let him pray?"

Unharmed beyond his brief choking, Lucifer said nothing as he looked between me and his daughter.

"I have a plan, if anyone wants to hear it," Deevi declared to the car as George took the exit for La Guardia. The streets were quiet and barren and the gray miles carried on.

Nobody spoke against her.

"When we get to the air...port?" She glanced at me for confirmation. I nodded a little. "When we get to the airport, I will leave this vehicle and do battle. I need you all to get away during that time and find our means of escape."

"That's your plan?" I asked, unenthused. "To fight your way through the archangels?"

She hummed her confirmation, giving me an affirmative nod.

"That's insane." George caught us in the rearview mirror as he navigated the concrete barricades separating the Escalade from the airport's constant construction. "They are creatures of omnipotent might that can bend time, space, and dimension itself."

"George," Merry hissed at him. "You can't say all that. They said we can't tell."

"Why bloody not?" he asked. "We're going to die the moment one of us gets out of this car, and maybe sooner. I'll not die a fool, nor a quiet one at that." George tried to keep steady, but his prideful expression broke. "Not for them."

"That is the second part of my plan. I will not go into battle alone," said Deevi. "Someone will have to keep the rooster safe."

"Why do we have to keep that chicken safe?" Merry asked, turning in the passenger seat.

"Because when you find our means of escape, I can repossess the rooster," Lucifer answered. "We might make an escape in time to avoid them tracking us."

"And who the hell is going to fly whatever plane we try to steal?" Merry questioned, more exasperated than before.

George sighed loudly in the driver's seat. "I can do it."

"Well, great," said Merry, crossing her arms as she faced forward.

Deevi addressed me. "Patrick, what do you think?"

"I've come up with far worse," I said.

"What's that?" Merry rose in her seat, against the seat belt that strapped her in. She braced her arms on the dash in panic. "George, drive!"

George slammed the gas. The Escalade's tires squealed as they caught pavement, and Deevi closed her arms around me to make sure I didn't move when the truck jerked forward.

A line of gunmen standing on the curb loosed their first chain of gunfire as we rumbled by. Bullets disintegrated the passenger side windows as Merry screamed in new terror. Shards fell upon Deevi where she lay atop of me. Lucifer crowed loudly, running to and fro between the seats while muttering obscenities in Enochian.

"Quiet," George screamed over them, hunched down in the seat so he could keep low. "Brace!"

The front end crashed through a fence gate. George had found us a way to the tarmac. We suddenly saw the planes at the endless terminals, and new panic hit me.

None of the jets moved. None of them took off, none taxied in or out of the runway—everything had stopped the moment we broke through.

Then shit got real. And sometimes real goes wrong.

Like a damned John Woo film, a row of black SUVs drove out from the closet terminal, approaching us in a perfect line right out of the GMC factory, red letters blazing. They all bore the white decals of a stationary cross on their hoods, and as we whipped by, I kept a bead on them to catch sight of their sides before they chased us.

I saw the title set on the black paint.

New Word Ministries.

"Like a fuck you for Christmas," I said aloud.

The Devil had gotten to La Guardia International before us.

3 8

THE WORST THING EVER

George popped the locks on the doors. "Now."

Yanking the sliding back door open, Deevi slipped from her place beside me on the middle bench. A rush of air followed by Lucifer's crowing. The rooster quieted immediately before unleashing a sharp cry. I dodged barbs and wings as the un-possessed bird simultaneously lost its shit on the carpet and seat, shoving his panicked beak away from my eyes.

The automatic hydraulics pulled the hatch closed while I corralled the bird without getting my hands cut up in the process, which proved near impossible when George swerved to avoid more gunfire.

Raphael's horn blew. A sudden clash of swords rose over the interplay of bullets.

"Hey! Hey, you see that? I—" George shouted while he drifted between two planes taxiing for takeoff, trapped in time. The roar of their engines vibrated the entire car and deafened me, leaving me unable to hear the rest of the words that came out of his mouth. Cacophony returned with his voice. "Merry, you see it?"

I lunged forward when the Escalade straightened. Getting my hands around the rooster's shanks in a stroke of pure timing, I laughed before another round of bullets struck the corner of the

Escalade. Tilted in my attempt to evade, I let go of the rooster and sat up to gain a view of the battlefield, an act that came with immediate, sincere regrets.

I followed the clock.

The sky flashed as thunder clouds rushed on our six. Heralded by a violent wind, the seven archangels had descended to earth from a gleaming hole in the sky after they had sounded the battle-horn. Two remained in the air, locked in a deadly clash of arms with Deevi. She engaged Uriel and Raphael above the tarmac. I lost sight of her as the three danced with blades of hard light, theirs white and hers the angry, angry red. They fought so quickly they vanished one moment only to reappear some place nearby the next, like fireflies in twilight.

The beauty dimmed when I realized she was trying to dive to earth. Her uncles prevented that decision, forcing her to break and struggle for altitude while they harried her from below.

Lucifer and Gabriel fought on our four o'clock, batting at each other with their swords while they appeared and disappeared like buzzing bees. Many of the New Word's number pulled over, the black-suited men getting out and leveling their rifles. The pair of archangels stopped their war and faced the new enemy when a fresh wall of bullets absorbed into their bodies and faces, perfectly still for a moment before they appeared behind Cromwell's men. They carved their way through bodies in ghastly displays of violence mortal man had no preparation to witness. The smart ones fled on foot to the terminal, running faster when both heavenly beings stalked after them.

I imagined every phone in the world by now had the news banner flashing across their screens. ANGELS IN NEW YORK.

"Oh, fuck," Merry screamed.

I faced toward noon in time to see us fly past Michael the Protector. The silver Sword of Truth at his side, he let us go by without a glance of attention. Merry and I both looked back, expecting him to be gone and reappear somewhere else. The rooster had hidden in the corner of the Escalade's rear, where he crowed like a loud, broken, annoying record.

"Where are the other two?" Merry shouted over the damned bird.

This time George screamed. "Oh, fuck!" He shoved the brakes down with his whole body. I nearly broke my arms keeping myself from being launched into the front of the car.

Before his own private G-550 readied in its own parking space, Satan marched toward the Escalade. He carried a sledgehammer, still in the wounded husk of Thomas Cromwell. I dug the shopping bag out from beneath Merry's seat, dumping it out before me. My and George's rosaries, our books, and our vestments fell out.

"Get out there," I said, handing George his stuff.

He opened the door without question, eager to meet the Devil as we had been raised.

"Tater, we're not going to survive this, are we?" Merry asked, motioning impatiently at one of her baskets from between the front and middle bench. Filled with her magics, I handed it to her, knowing she would figure something out.

I followed George without an answer, hoping that God would spare her and the rooster.

George ducked the first swipe of the hammer as we met our foe, dropping low into a sweep that knocked out one of Satan's legs. I caught the bastard around the middle before he rebalanced, driving him hard into the cement beneath us. Knee to his chest, I rose up and belted him twice in the face.

Satan smiled up at me, white teeth smeared in his host's blood. "I don't got a rock in my mouth now, boy."

"Good, you can say your prayers." I opened my left hand and slapped my rosary to the side of his false face. Cromwell's flesh burned beneath the cross. Through the sear against my own skin I held, waiting for George to come in with the spiel. He arrived, smacking the back of his Bible against Satan's nose, which crushed it in one fell swoop. I hopped up and stood beside him. We whipped our rosaries around our hands like the MacManus boys.

George started, his Bible out in front of him as gunfire roared behind us. "Our Father, who art in Heaven, hallowed be thy name—"

I flipped open to Isaiah. "Forget the former things; do not dwell on the past! See, I am doing a new thing! Now it springs up; do you not perceive it? I am making a way in the wilderness and streams in the wasteland!"

The Devil writhed before us, trapped by the holy power of God's words.

A baggage car rolled past us in a booming clatter, tumbling like a desert weed from an old West movie while the flames engulfed it. For some reason, I turned to check behind me. I can't say why, but I knew I needed to bear witness.

Michael and Lucifer stood face to face with Gabriel between them.

They weren't tearing each other apart.

Nothing good could come from that.

High above, Deevi warred against Uriel while Raphael retreated, his crimson robes streaked darker in places while he favored his sword arm. Swords of heaven and fury shed lightning every time they came together. Titans beat upon each other's guards until one forced an opening or the other gave in, the work of divine wills in a battle beyond comprehension.

"Patrick, what are you doing?" George shouted before it was too late.

The Devil smacked me hard in the side with his sledge, sending me rolling with rib-breaking force. My head cracked the ground with a pop.

The world faded in and out, from breath to breath.

The hammer struck the cement with echoing force. Merry screamed before the darkness took me.

STILL THE WORST

Somehow I got my feet under me in the middle of the melee, wobbling as I tried to steady a tortured, labored breath from planting me back on my knees. Fire spread across the left side of my body. My arm curled against my direction. I could feel the broken ends of at least two ribs shift. Knives of hot, hot anger pierced me.

Satan swung at George a few feet away from me, who ducked like a veteran of a thousand sword fights he didn't fight in this life. He dove in when the possessed body of Thomas Cromwell overextended, grabbing the sledgehammer's handle.

On instinct and adrenaline alone, I ran and threw myself hard into a straight front kick at Satan's spine, which snapped like a pine two-by-four.

The bastard didn't go down.

Satan ripped his weapon from his tussle with George and whipped around. His torso led first, followed by his legs which made weird crunching noises when they righted themselves in the proper direction. I felt the wind of the hammer's head brush the top of my skull as I ducked, rolling hard to the point of numbing my ribs and accepting the torture God placed on the menu for the day.

Agony stopped that stupid idea. I crumpled on my side, unable to move again.

Holding the fifteen-pound sledge up in one hand like it weighed nothing, the Devil smiled an impossibly wide smile, his black eyes gleaming like draining stars. "Batter up."

I wheezed out the beginnings of a freestyle. "By the holiness of the Virgin, I speak to thee, demon of Hell! Lay down your weapon and return to Perdition, for God has seen thine grotesqueness and deemed you ill!"

It made him wince.

George started proper. "Our Father, who art in heaven..." He rattled off the basics, jerking Satan in his direction for an instant as I tried my best to conjure up some old Scottish shit for casting out evil. One had to love the Scots. Not only did they add half to the venerable Scotch-Irish, but they knew how to deal with otherworldly things.

They dealt with them the hard way.

"I stand behind the armor of Michael, Guard of Heaven. Behind his shield I am protected from the blows of my enemies, and from his arm I shall strike back out and take from you what you intend of me!" I dribbled the end of my rosary out of my hand, the silver cross clean beneath the stormy skies Deevi's battle with her uncles had produced. Somehow, by some will beyond mine, I rose to my knees. "Begone, unclean thing, from heather and heath, and tread no hoof upon God's good earth! Begone! Begone!"

Satan flung the sledge at George, who sidestepped easily, and then he came at me. Merry and the rooster cried in the background.

Too terrified to do little more than hear the crash of the hammer through the Escalade's back window, my eyes never left his form. He descended upon me, an unnatural strength imbuing Cromwell's thin, athletic, but broken frame. I tried to keep away, but he punched me so hard in the face, I blacked out.

His next punch woke me up.

My brain somehow decided to drive my heel into a kick that tagged him right on the point of his chin. Halted, he leered before

George launched himself on Satan's back, arms hooked tight to his neck for a deep rear choke.

Satan reared back, grabbing George's closest elbow and forearm. Terrified he'd rip the Dragonslayer's arm off, I curled my leg against my body's protest and drove my heel into his balls with all my might.

Then I blacked out again.

I woke up with my ass in the air and cement rasping the side of my face.

Getting to all fours, every limb shook while I tried to force myself to stay awake. The ringing in my ears forced my eyes shut. I was bleeding inside. The sickening weight, the torpor of death, slowed every movement I tried to make.

George remained atop of it, getting the verse out when he could. "I banish you, Shaytan, back to your place in Perdition! Go, and do not tarry in the world of God's children again."

I willed myself to open my eyes, in time to see the Devil fling George against the crumpled side of the Escalade. My friend crashed to the ground, unconscious as blood ran from his mouth.

Somehow I rose to my feet once more.

Satan walked over to the dented, damaged truck. Laying a hand on the exposed handle of the hammer sticking through the Escalade's broken back window, he looked down at George as he lifted it out.

"No, you don't," I hissed out, unable to find my breath. My right arm wrapped around my ribs as I thrust out my Bible with the left, the only thing left for me to do. The Devil cocked his head in my direction, a fluid twist of his head. The shadow of his demonic face crawled under his human mask.

"Our Father, who art in Heaven, hallowed be thy name—" I started.

The lord of demons turned to face me. "That shit gets very annoying."

I dodged his first downward stroke when he loomed over me. Rolling to the side, I landed on my back with a groan and kicked the hardest I could muster at his kneecap. Satan or no Satan, the rules of a meat suit applied. The blow collapsed out his left leg from under him, long enough for me to crawl away before he came around low with the hammer. In time to save my legs, I tried to push myself on the rough pavement, unable to defeat the friction of my clothes against the old concrete.

Satan rose, no worse for wear.

Seeing the black composite handle just below the polished steel block as it swung down at me, I sagged left in time to take the former over the latter in a shot on my left side. In boxing they taught us to roll with a blow, but they always cautioned that there was only so much punishment one could take.

Damage damaged, no matter how one took it.

I took every inch of that handle. The sting throughout my torso seized me, and my legs flailed as my body skipped across the cement like a stone.

Oh, fuck, I thought:

I was about to meet my maker. I didn't expect it to go well.

Light flashed in my vision. I readied for the last breath, the last feel of my skin on my bones.

I may have cried.

I didn't say goodbye to Deevi. I didn't have the time.

I did cry.

The flashed ended. I gasped on La Guardia's tarmac, laying where I had fallen. The sear of my broken body coursed through my nervous system into a wail that I'm not sure I made aloud. Yet for the fire, the sear, I noticed an odd peace had fallen upon the earth.

The stormy skies had parted to a central beam of undiluted light.

God had come to earth.

Because fuck me, right?

40

"BAH GAWD, HE HAS A STEEL CHAIR!"

I had never seen the world truly still.

God shone upon the earth, bathing everything in his gaze in a force beyond imagination's imagination, beyond time and space, and everything else. It all froze in perfect sync, as if someone had paused the video game. I lay on my back, frozen against the cement as every nerve screamed for release from my broken body. Trapped in reality, there'd be no end until the Lord allowed it.

The light spread across the tarmac, on the archangels first, who landed in a perfect line to bow their heads before their creator.

Only then did I get a glimpse of Lucifer in all his glory.

Decked in a shimmering breastplate of ancient design, his bright sword glistened as he balanced its point against the ground, bared but not raised in threat. Golden haired and like-eyed, he did not flinch when glory struck his face, staring back with defiance.

Raphael and Uriel sandwiched God's first, and I wondered where Deevi had gone in the fray.

I quickly discovered my answer.

Deevi flew for me, diving from the sky like a hawk for a mouse.

God's beams flashed after her, following her path. Considering what he did to the last batch of Nephilim, the light did not bode happiness. No matter how fast she stroked the static air, he overtook her before I could blink.

The light passed over me next.

I hoped for oblivion. Blinded, I held my breath, ready to be freed.

When I came to, I was on my feet without a shred of pain.

So were George and Deevi, standing there on the tarmac looking around like something had stolen something from each of them. Taking in the battlefield, I spotted Merry still sitting in the passenger seat of the Escalade. She hunched over, either in terror or working on something, but she lived.

And so did Satan, though he did not seem to understand why.

Between George and I, he grasped at sections of his suited body. "No... You've trapped me again. Again," he said in a low, animalistic voice while he searched his persons. His unsettled glare roamed toward God's light. Wielding the hammer, the demonic face beyond Cromwell's human one emerged. A great horned general, he pointed his weapon at the hole in the sky. "We shall war forever, no matter how many I have to take!"

The beams of illumination redirected at Satan once more, striking his chest. A sonic boom clapped the air.

Blown backwards, the Devil flew right past the point where he had started and slammed into the side of the battered Escalade. Bits of glass sticking from his back, Satan pressed himself from the man-shaped dent, bloody rents torn from his shoulders and neck.

"Oh, fuck," I said.

Not the first words I should have chosen to speak right after God had restored me.

The Lord's light seeped, the clouds in the sky spinning around the pinhole from heaven in a counter-clockwise motion. As quickly as God came, he left, no words of wisdom or hope passing to his flock.

And the dragon still roamed.

Satan went for George as Deevi stepped in front of the possessed vessel. Her burning sword held in both hands, she swung before he lifted his sledge. The head of Thomas Cromwell came off without a bubble of blood, the stump cauterized. The body dropped to the side as it lost all life.

Suddenly the passenger side door of the Escalade opened. Merry ran around the front holding a small, brown ring between her finger and thumb. "Found it," she announced proudly, before her gaze invariably lowered to the decapitated head near her feet.

Cromwell's black eyes popped open.

Merry screamed bloody murder.

The detached body hopped to its feet like nothing had happened, fists clenched at its side in a battle pose.

Deevi charged in, striking out at the headless body. The Devil's corpse dodged expertly, controlled by a center of gravity not constrained by the weight of a head. Her blade burned the air with a crackle every time she missed, followed by a deep, guttural sound she made on the follow up. They danced away, chasing each other in a dangerous game of tag.

"Not even the power of God can destroy me," Satan's head cried out. "I am the true Alpha and Omega! The scourge of the Platinum Polis! The king of Perdition! Mine is the everlasting!"

The rooster, on cue, leapt from one of the Escalade's exposed windows. Feathers all in a tizzy, Lucifer shouted in his deep, cawing voice. "Exorcise the head, you fools!"

A quick check to my right, I spotted the seven archangels on the march in our direction. "George!"

He scuttled forward from where he stood and collected the sledgehammer before I could say anything else. "On it!"

Merry ran back around the front of the Escalade. "I'll get my gun!"

"You've had a gun?" I asked before she disappeared beyond my view.

"Saint Patrick!" the rooster cawed.

I spotted Cromwell's severed head, shouting his curses upon creation. Grabbing him by his hair, I held the heavy lump by a handful of crisp, conditioned locks.

"I fucking bite your nuts off, saint," he screamed at me.

"What the fuck," I muttered, unfurling my green-beaded rosary I had been clutching in my left hand. "Demon, I beseech, in the name of the Holy Mother, who bore our son in darkness before his light entered the world—be gone, Shaytan! Begone from this man's form that you defile! Leave, Shaytan, and return to the mire you call your own!"

Somehow using the momentum of his jaw alone, the demon bit my wrist. I dropped the son of a bitch right on the noggin, which made a loud knock that brought me some hope the bastard had died then and there.

The head rolled to the side. The demon glanced up at me and blew a raspberry.

Lucifer sprinted at the severed head and pecked at its face, stepping around the forehead to get better angles at the eyes. The demon screamed as the tiny yellow beak perforated his cheeks and brow, tearing at the whites until blood wept from the pulped mess.

"Say your name, fiend!" a red-faced Lucifer demanded to know between digs, his brown hackles raised. "Speak!"

"You have no control over me, Noble One," the gross head roared. "You despot! Down with despots!"

"We don't have time, demon," I cried, holding my rosary against the remaining cheek on its face, the blood from the rest drenching my hand. "In the name of Christ, who died on the cross so that you, who are unworthy, may know the truth and light! It pierces you and your evil, demon! Reveal your name, or it shall pierce you again!"

The heat under my palm scorched.

The demon opened its rotten, yellow-toothed mouth and howled in agony.

Stabilized by my hand clutching Cromwell's head by what stump there was, Lucifer dug one of his barbs into a dead eye. "You shall fall to the glory of the high! In the name of Creation, you shall reveal yourself to those who mastered souls! Speak, demon, so we might send you to your darkness!"

"The Word resides in her," the demon shrieked. "And the Word will be made new!"

Michael the Protector spoke next. "Are you two done yet?"

I flinched at the archangel's voice and turned, face to face with the point of the Protector's silver sword. I don't know how I breathed past the ozone radiating off the tip, but somehow I got in enough air to keep myself from hyperventilating. Perfectly still, I moved not an inch.

"You're wasting time, Lucifer," he said, his bright eyes bored into mine as he held the point before my nose. "You've been given orders."

"You expect too much of humans," the rooster said, out of eye shot. "And no matter the time, Patrick's duty is his duty! I shall not impede it."

"You could also just not point that in my face," I said.

Michael lifted his glowing blade, setting it on the shimmering cloth wrapped over his shoulder. "Be quick. We will secure your transportation."

"What?" I asked, unsure of what I had heard.

Lucifer crowed at me. "Patrick!"

"Right," I said, looking down at the head by my knees. The demon let out an impossible hiss of air, the silver crucifix of my rosary rested on his forehead. God still worked to save this man.

Resigned to my duty, I laid my hand on Cromwell's rotting forehead. "I beseech thee, demon, to flee from this vessel that houses God's child. Flee, I say to thee, back to the darkness of your abode, where you shall await judgment beside your fallen ilk. Say your name to me, demon, and I shall free you before you are forced to give up your purchase on this man's being."

The buzz of a plane interrupted my concentration as the Gulfstream 550, the transatlantic kind only rich people like Cromwell could afford off his tithes, wheeled its way toward me. The door to the cabin open, Merry held her silver .38 against the base of the stewardess's neck, cussing at her in ways I thankfully could not hear over the whine of the engines.

To my shock, Saint George the Dragonslayer and Gabriel the Messenger helmed the cockpit.

"Hurry," said Michael.

"You shall not defeat me! The New Word shall be spoken," cried the severed head.

"Leave, you who shrieks in the light of God," I intoned. "Call out not the name of your sullied lord, who slinks into shadow at the mere mention of Jehovah! Do not cling to innocent life, for the Lord's light is upon you, and you shall be punished for every moment you wither! Say thy name, demon, and preserve thyself in Perdition!"

The noise of the plane drowned out the rest of my words, but I threw in a few Hail Marys and Our Fathers.

Strangely, the thought of Mary gave me solace. God didn't tell her anything either before everything went to south for her, her husband, and her wee boy. I tried to force the image of the maiden into my mind, thinking back on statues and Da Vinci paintings, and somewhere, for some reason, Deevi.

She tore the last piece of Cromwell's wriggling body apart in the distance, yet another desecration allowed by Satan's cruelty.

I covered the demon's face with my hand. "Speak your name so that you may see light, demon, and I promise you she will be kind.".

The demon answered, rasping every word. "I see her... My name..."

"Tell her your name, demon," I said, recalling the gentleness that caused the rest of them I had met in this mad chase to move on. "Go in peace instead of peril, for the Lord God will judge this moment, too."

"Shaytan," the demon whispered, bitter to the end.

"In the name of God, Shaytan, spare this soul your burden."

The severed face calmed, its eyes shut, like a man who hadn't suffered a beating, dismemberment, a holy object burnt to his flesh, let alone the decapitation. Cromwell passed from this earth to whatever judgment lay next for him. He mouthed the Virgin's name before he expired in my hands.

Michael vanished in a heartbeat.

So did everything else. The bodies of the dead, the ruined Escalade. Like it had never happened.

Leaving nothing there on the tarmac, I turned and sprinted for the descending staircase lowering from the Gulfstream. Lucifer ran behind me, flapping his feathered wings to stand grounded against the currents. Quickly outpacing him, I stopped short of the steps and let the plane roll by.

I don't know why, but I turned and crouched down. To my further surprise the rooster leapt into my open arms. I scampered up the steps, cradling my former possessor like a cherished pet.

Because why the fuck not at this point?

41

THE LAST PHONE CALL

I woke on the cream leather couch in the Gulfstream's main cabin somewhere over the Atlantic. George had gotten us to altitude quickly, and after waiting a full hour for the National Guard to shoot us down, or a dragon to fall from the sky, or demons to rip off the door and fight us tooth and nail, we could finally rest. The moment I realized that I passed out on the nearest flat surface that fit me.

Merry was sitting at the other end of the couch when I opened my eyes, giving me a tired smile. Wrapped in a fine knit blanket, she curled against the furniture's contours like a cat. "Hey, Tater."

A quick scan of the cabin revealed that we were the only ones in it. George sat up front in the cockpit, visible past the open door. Deevi and Lucifer had gone back into the bedroom.

Barefoot, I scooted up on the couch and started to rub the sleep from my eyes. "How long was I out?"

Merry watched me yawn. "About three hours."

We sat there while the world rushed by the plane outside, the muted currents captured in the silence between her and I.

I brought my feet up on the couch. She pressed hers forward, touching her toes with mine like we used to.

I swallowed in the low light of the cabin. "I'm sorry, Merry."

"I know, Tater. I forgive you."

I didn't know what more to say. I had torn demons from the souls of men, women, children, one claw at a time. I had watched mothers scream while they climbed the walls of infirmaries. I had once punched the Devil right in the face, and even that paled in comparison to everything that had happened in the last week.

At least I hadn't been ripped into another dimension.

My hand reached out for hers. Merry threaded her fingers with mine. She cried.

I wondered how fucked George was.

I wanted to crawl inside myself, God, and not do this anymore.

Why had this happened? Why all the secrets?

Why didn't you speak to me? Why didn't you tell me what I needed to do so I could save my friends from what happened?

I needed someone to tell me it was going to be okay so I could show Merry that. And Deevi. And George.

If not me, why not for them?

A buzzing interrupted our quiet.

Tossed on the side table with the rest of our lighters, keys, Merry's surprise gun, clothes, and every other little bit of trash that had gotten in our pockets, my burner rattled on the polished cherry top.

"How high are we?" I asked her.

"I don't know, Tater," Merry said. "All I know is that I'm not high enough for that."

Crossing the cabin, I looked at the screen and stopped.

The Chair called.

I tapped the green icon and put the phone to my ear, half-expecting to hear demons speak on the other end. "Hello?"

"Is that you, Saint Patrick?"

Part of me still wondered if this was a trick, hearing that nice old Argentinian tremble on the other end of the line. The last week fell back on my shoulders while the tight cords of sleep unbound from my brain. "It's me, your Holiness. It is good to hear your voice."

The Chair let out a tired laugh. "Well, God is good to both of us it seems."

"Where are you? What happened after Rome?"

"The Swiss Guard was able to get me to a secret passage that led outside the Vatican's walls during the attack. Thank God we are safe, and hopefully in this place they have brought me to that will remain the case. Where are you?"

"Headed to Dublin."

"Is the angel still with you?"

I glanced toward the closed door to the bedroom. "She's safe."

The Chair paused on the other end of the line. "What support can I give you, Saint Patrick?"

"Support, your Holiness?" Merry and I locked eyes. She tilted her head to the side, lips parted in an unspoken question. "At this point, I just want to get to Ireland."

"The resources of the Church and whatever we can provide will be yours."

I nodded while watching Merry's expression turn in confusion. "I have George with me. May I hand him the phone?"

"Please," said the Chair. "God has blessed us indeed to have you both of you safe and sound!"

I couldn't have hated God more in that moment than I did. Keeping words to myself that the old man didn't deserve, I forced my tone steady. "Call back in five minutes?"

"Of course, Saint Patrick," said the Chair. "And God bless you."

I failed to make any sort of pleasant farewell, mashing my thumb on the red dot in the center of the glass face. "Fuck."

"Who was that?" Merry asked, sitting up on the beige cream couch with concern.

"Oh, just the Pope."

Her brown eyes widened to the size of bottle caps. "And you told him we're headed toward Ireland?"

"I told him we're headed to Dublin. Be right back."

I left her there wondering as I had too many times, exhaustion and frustration cutting off the answers I should have tried for. I knocked on the cockpit's door frame.

"Enter," George called from within.

I slid through the hole into the cockpit. George sat in the pilot's chair, his hands slack on the wheel and his shoes kicked off while he rested his feet on the rudder pedals. He stared out the front windscreen, an endless darkness beaded in droplets on the glass. The blue light of the heads-up display clashed with the red glow from the board.

"Storm?" I asked.

"Just rain." He kept staring, his words dry and hollow.

Oh fuck, God. Look at what we did. The console between us glowed silently, the lights outlining the switches and knobs revealing the haggard edges of George's face and the emptiness of his expression.

I squeezed the phone in my hand, unsure if I was about to do the right thing. "The Chair called."

A flicker of life lit in his gray eyes. "The Chair?"

"He's alive," I said. "Hiding somewhere. He's going to call back in a few minutes to talk to you."

The patron saint of England chewed on that news for a few seconds before he nodded. He held out his hand.

I put the phone in it. "Can I ask you to do something, if we can do it?"

"What do you want, Patrick?"

"I need you land us around Shannon—not Dublin. But tell them Dublin. Set it up on the call."

He glanced at me, then the phone, and slowly nodded. We both knew the truth.

We were alone now and not even the Vatican could be trusted.

"It'll save us on fuel," he said. "Know any good landing strips if I can't get us into the airport?"

"There's an old highway I can probably find with some time on the Wi-Fi." I looked around his space. "Fucking hell, how are we going to get rid of this thing?"

George didn't answer. Smoothly his gaze drifted from me back to the night outside, where wind and wet thrashed in oblivion.

4 2

THE LORD'S WORK

I shut the door to the cockpit behind me and turned, freezing on the spot when I saw them.

Gabriel the Messenger stood over the couch where Merry slept, the priestess curled beneath a blanket while the rain outside played a slow, calming beat against the jet. Their bright white wings, drawn tight to accommodate their adjusted height, matched the intensity of the pink curls that fell around their face like vines.

The archangel looked my way. "Hello, Saint Patrick," they said, staking me on the spot.

"Get away from her," I braved to say.

"You're a good man, Saint Patrick." The archangel gave me a sad smile and nodded. "I'd respond the same way if I were in your position."

"But you're not. Why are you here?" I asked.

"I come with the Word."

Fuck you.

"I heard that," Gabriel said.

My rage lurched me forward. "How dare he send you and demand—"

They faced me, not moving an inch when I bowed up to them. "Please, Patrick—"

"No," I shouted. Fuck it, everyone needed to wake up. "What does he want this time? To send us off towards death again, right? Or maybe, instead of trying to save Deevi, we need to have that baby, right? What about George? Does he need to go kill someone again? What about her?" I said, gesturing at my former lover who remained strangely inert. "Does another human soul need to be spent so you can have your fucking mystery?"

The archangel shuddered. "I know this hasn't been easy."

I stood there, fists balled to throw. "You took—"

They lifted a hand to quiet me. "I didn't want to take them. Michael did that, and—"

"You still took them." I looked at Merry spread out on the couch. She hadn't awoken.

In fact, she didn't breathe. A check on the window beyond revealed a flash of thunder that speared the clouds many miles off, caught like the snapping bulb of an old camera. Even the rain had ceased its lashing of the plane, leaving us in uninterrupted peace.

We hung miles above the ocean.

"I stopped time," Gabriel answered.

"Of course you did," I said through gritted teeth.

The bedroom door opened.

Deevi stood in the space, her golden eyes shining in the dark of the room. She stepped through, followed by her wings until she cleared the doorway. To my great shock, Lucifer snoozed in the midst of a deep sleep, tucked under her arm.

Gabriel smiled at their niece. "I see my little lesson worked."

"He fell right asleep like you said he would, Auntie Gabriel," Deevi whispered.

The celestials shared a secret smile, one they did not hide from me.

"It always worked." Gabriel reached forward with their perfect hand and touched Lucifer's single red comb. Their wavering sadness disappeared, replaced by that firm, compassionate gaze art and artists had reflected throughout history. "I shall be quick. The Lord has heard your prayers, Patrick."

Shit.

"Indeed," she said, unable to hide more of that clever grin. "Go to Ireland. You shall find your task there."

I barely contained the spite in my voice. "Get fucked."

"Patrick," Deevi said, leaning to the side to look past Gabriel's wings.

"Let him be," Gabriel said. "That was all I was told to say. What you do from thereon is your business, Saint Patrick, but I hope you will be the man who does the business I know he is meant to do." Gabriel gave Lucifer, then Deevi, one last loving glance before they let their blazing eyes drift to the ceiling. "Bye."

Rain and wind roared alive the split second the archangel popped out of the world. The flash of thunder disappeared as the jet continued at its original speed, no longer bound by divine distortion. Merry and Lucifer still slept, no worse for wear or knowing what had happened—an honest blessing given how it could have gone if they had woken up.

"So you and Gabriel talk?" I asked, blunt about it.

Deevi attempted to speak when her father's sleepy-time bock interrupted her. Blowing me a silent "shush", she laid the rooster down by Merry's feet on the airline couch. She wagged her finger for me to follow her to the bedroom.

Not in the mood in the least, I trudged behind her, shuffling like a kid being dragged to confession.

She pointed me to the bed, where I sat on its foot. She shut the door to the sleepers in the main compartment. My hands in my lap, I stared at the white shag.

She put her first two fingers of her right hand under my chin and lifted. "Patrick."

I looked her dead in the eyes. "Dear."

For the first time since I found her in that basement, Deevi closed her eyes for a moment in exhaustion. Unexpected lines creased her face. "During the battle between Lucifer, myself, and the archangels,

Gabriel disappeared. Not even Michael knew where they went. They reappeared moments later with a direct edict from God. Being the Messenger all took their word for truth. Even Michael."

"And what did God say?" I asked, trying hard not to sigh at the news.

Deevi held my face tight. "Do you really want to know?"

Compelled to the truth, I answered without hesitation. "Not in the least."

"Why not?" she asked, her brows popped in surprise.

"Because I don't want to hear about God right now. I don't want to hear about God, or angels, or the Devil, or evangelicals. I don't want to even think about Heaven or Hell ever again if I don't have to. I don't want to do a damn bloody thing with God ever again."

"Not even me?" she had to ask.

"Oh, Deevi," I said, breaking into tears. "I'd never wish to be away from you."

I cried. She held me. I don't know how long I cried for, but I knew I cried loud enough that Merry and the rooster probably heard me.

None of it mattered.

I kept calling to you, God, and you never answered. You sent your flunkies.

I had slapped the taste out of the Devil's mouth, drove the serpents from Eire, walked through Purgatory to rescue who you wanted rescued, and still died poor, penniless, and unable to save my first wife, who died of a goddamn cold because I was dying of it too. Apparently, I agreed to come back here, to this real perdition of sin and suffering, to spread your work again, casting out things a hundred times worse than the first batch of snakes.

And still, you sent your flunkies.

I didn't want thanks. I knew that wasn't the business we were in. I just needed to know what I could do to do better.

And yet you still asked me to find a new task?

And you sent a flunky?

I'm just a flunky too, I guess.

I cried and cried and cried for hours until I fell asleep. The smaller spoon to Deevi and her wings, I lay upon the bed caught between the bliss of her and the sufferings you created from the seat of your throne.

Your goddamned throne. Another fucking royal telling Irish souls how to die.

"Patrick."

I opened my eyes when she pulled up the window-cover, revealing the blue dawn beyond. The sun turned the horizon bright gold, and I rose from the bed energized like I hadn't been in a long, long time.

Eire.

Outside the glass the Shannon Estuary gleamed beyond the emerald hills, which seemed to glimmer like their namesakes in the wee hours of the morning. George turned the plane in for its descent, and I sat back down on the bed, clutching my heart in anticipation.

I had found my way home. I had done it.

Deevi bowled me over on the bed. She pinned me as she laughed aloud in complete happiness, her wings' weight holding us down as the Gulfstream leveled out.

"Look what you did, Saint Patrick," she whispered in my face, those golden eyes my only vision. "You kept your promise." She kissed my lips once, twice, before a tear trailed down to the point of her nose, wetting mine when they touched. "You're the only person to keep their word to me."

She kissed me more as George lowered the landing gear. I heard the rooster crowing beyond the door.

We touched down on a back road in sunny County Clare. Even before I stepped off the plane to touch Ireland's soil, bittersweetness overwhelmed me.

I still thanked you, God, for the fact I had made it home.

THE END

ACKNOWLEDGMENTS

Everything I do is for Margo and Ben.

I want to thank John Hartness for always believing in me. Erin Penn deserves huge credit in helping me put this manuscript together in a cogent fashion, as does Sarah Adams. I need to thank Samuel Montgomery-Blinn, JD Blackrose, and Ziggy Nixon for their words and encouragement. I owe my parents a lot, most of all for always raising me in a safe, open household where inquiry was allowed. There are too many writers before me to thank, but let's go with Garth Ennis, Kevin Smith, and Clive Barker.

I also need to thank Reverand Wormley of St. Mark's Evangelical Lutheran Church in St. Louis, Missouri, who made me believe I had the Devil in me when I was seven because that's what they do to children. Bad move, padre.

I also need to thank the people who cannot be named for the sake of jobs and security, which include clergy, parishioners, and former members of the Holy Roman Catholic Church who were kind enough to offer words, debates, questions, and also encouragement. A lot of good people are fighting a good fight and feel alone in it because of the institution where they reside. Always remember that there are good people wherever you look for them, including in the places these stories take aim at like the Vatican. I also want to acknowledge Pope Francis, who is moving heaven and earth to cleanse the many sins of his church. I also need to thank Dr. James Tabor, Dr. Jeremy Schott, and Dr. Sean McCloud of the Religious Studies program at the University of North Carolina at Charlotte. I also need to make a special mention of David Hayward, aka The Naked Pastor, who's art and worldview played a dramatic role in these novels.

Finally, I want to thank Jesus Christ and the founders of his movement. I read the Bible so many times in its many different variations (including the books that were left out) before and during the writing of these novels that I could not help but listen, and in listening I found profound safety, courage, and love. Please bless my child and all children.

ABOUT THE AUTHOR

Raised in the hills of North Carolina and Maryland, Jay Requard is a graduate of The University of North Carolina at Charlotte with a degree in History and Religious Studies. An award-winning author of Epic Fantasy, Sword & Sorcery, and Urban Fantasy, he is also the host of Pondering The Orb on YouTube. In his free time, he enjoys wandering, reading, and cooking for his wife, son, and a small star-cat named Mona Underfoot. They reside in New York City.

Find out more about Jay and his books at jayrequard.com.

ALSO BY JAY REQUARD

Atenia (Epic Fantasy)

A Wave of Lions (Epic Fantasy/Sword & Sorcery), which include the following titles:

The Curse of Shallow Bay

At the Mirror's Edge

The Queen in Silver

Death & Dust: The Pale Sand Adventures (Dark Fantasy)

Spy/Counter/Killer (Sword & Sorcery), which include the following titles:

A Dangerous Brew

A Spirited Blend

A Spot Before Dead

War Pigs (Sword & Sorcery)

FRIENDS OF FALSTAFF

Thank You to all our Falstaff Books Patrons, who get extra digital content each month! To be featured here and see what other great rewards we offer, go to www.patreon.com/falstaffbooks.

PATRONS

Dino Hicks
John Hooks
John Kilgallon
Larissa Lichty
Travis & Casey Schilling
Staci-Leigh Santore
Sheryl R. Hayes
Scott Norris
Samuel Montgomery-Blinn
Junkle

www.ingramcontent.com/pod-product-compliance
Lightning Source LLC
Chambersburg PA
CBHW050315110726
47899CB00007B/2251